GODS OF MAGIC

DRAGON'S GIFT: THE AMAZON BOOK 1

LINSEY HALL

To Neil and Yoshi, with love.

1

THE ALLEY STANK OF DARK MAGIC AND DEATH. I CROUCHED BEHIND a trash can with my sister Bree, trying to breathe shallowly. Black magic swirled on the air, almost invisible but obvious from its stench.

"Remind me what the heck we're doing here, Rowan?" Bree asked.

"You keep poking into my business, so I'll show you." I peered out onto the darkened street. We were in The Vaults, the underground dark magic district of Edinburgh. The twisty-turny cobblestone streets were located right below Edinburgh Castle, and if one were inclined, they could find all manner of dark magic there.

But I wasn't inclined to find dark magic.

I was inclined to find a murderer.

I shifted, trying to keep my black leather boots out of the mucky puddle, and debated if we should actually be on a different street altogether.

"How'd you know to come here?" Bree whispered from beside me. "Doesn't look particularly murderous."

Without removing my gaze from the street, I dug into my

pocket and withdrew the little slip of paper, then passed it to Bree.

This had to be the correct alley. Right?

Paper rustled as Bree opened the note. I could hear the frown in her voice. "It says to come to the crossroads of Evil and Despair, and there you will stop a murder." I glanced over to see her gaze shoot toward mine. Her dark hair glinted in the light, and her black leather jacket helped her blend with the shadows, just like mine did. "Who the heck sent this to you?"

Actually, that was a second mystery I needed to figure out. "I don't know. But I can't ignore it, can I?"

She frowned. "No, I guess not."

"Exactly."

"But it's dangerous."

I shot her a scowl. Bree had so much magic that she was basically a god. A Dragon God who had fully come into her power, to be precise. She had been gifted the powers of the Norse gods, a transaction made possible by dragon magic. She had more than a dozen powers. Our world was full of magic, and Bree was one of the most gifted of all.

Me?

Not so much.

I had basically no power—not anymore, at least—but that didn't mean I'd turn away from something dangerous. *Especially* if it meant stopping a murder.

My glare worked, and Bree got the point. Contrition flashed on her face. "Sorry."

"I know." She worried because she loved me, but it still stung. Not only did I have Bree, my mega-powerful sister, I also had Ana, my *second* mega-powerful sister. I loved them so much that I'd die for them, but it was still a little tough to live in their shadows.

I shoved the thought way.

That way lay madness. And I wasn't here to mope about my crappy magic. I was here to stop a murder.

Only two people could possibly know a crime was about to go down—the perpetrator or a seer. I really hoped my info came from a seer.

I fingered the dagger strapped to my thigh and frowned. *The crossroads of Evil and Despair*, the note had said. "This street is named Evil and this alley is called Despair, but I don't think it's the right location."

"How do you know?" Bree asked.

"Just feels wrong. Too quiet." Maybe it was instinct. I had pretty good instincts after learning how to operate in a magical world without magic.

Unbeknownst to humans, the world was full of magic. Shifters, Magica, vampires, and demons all existed right under their noses, either walking in disguise or sticking to all-magic cities and neighborhoods. The Great Peace, the most powerful bit of magic ever created, hid us from human eyes. They could see us but not our magic—which we tried not to use around them anyway.

Edinburgh had one of the biggest all-magic neighborhoods in the world, located right in the Grassmarket. The Vaults, where we were currently located, was situated right next to the Grassmarket and stuffed full to the gills with dark magic and questionable individuals.

"Don't you have class in the morning?" Bree asked. "Should you be out so late?"

I scowled at her. "Off topic."

"Not really. You're about to officially start at the Undercover Protectorate's Academy of Magic, and you can't miss class."

I huffed. The Undercover Protectorate was a secret organization dedicated to protecting vulnerable supernaturals and keeping magic in check. My two sisters and I lived at their castle headquarters in the Scottish Highlands, and they were both full members. Six months ago, Bree and Ana rescued me from five years of captivity—just the memory made me shudder—so I lived there with them.

To fully join the Protectorate, you had to pass their Academy. The only reason I even had a chance at starting at the Academy was because Bree and Ana had gone there and done so well.

Except I currently had no magic, so I was the pity add.

I'd done a few informal classes there, but tomorrow was my first full, official day. Considering that I'd lost all my power during my captivity, class was going to be a doozy. I was damned good with weapons and potions and never, ever gave up, but even that wasn't going to get me through.

I ignored the thought and focused on the street in front of me. On the possible murder that was about to occur.

This I could control. With my actions here, maybe I could do some good.

"I won't miss class," I said. "And I have to do this."

"This isn't the first note you've gotten, is it?" Bree asked.

"No. I've gotten a few others, slipped right under my door. The first was a robbery. I thought it was crap, but it wasn't. I went to the assigned place and time, and stopped old Mr. Amos from having all his pygmy toads stolen."

"The old guy who has the shop at the entrance to The Vaults?"

"Yep. Then it was stopping an arms deal, and a black magic mob beating. But this is the first time one of the notes said murder." And now I was definitely sure we were at the wrong place. It'd been too long, and it was too quiet. I stood. "Come on. We've got to try Option B."

"What's that?" Bree whispered as we hurried out onto the street.

"There's a shop called Evil and a bar called Despair located right on a little square at the back of The Vaults. Maybe it'll happen there."

"You sure know this place well," Bree said.

It'd taken a lot of practice to learn the ins and outs of The Vaults, but it had paid off. *I'm still alive, right?*

But there was another reason, too, one I didn't want to share. Not even with my sister.

I liked the place. Something in the darkened streets reached into my soul and soothed. I *shouldn't* have liked such a place, one that was full of dark magic and evil.

But I did.

I hadn't always been that way. On bad nights, I thought that something in my soul was changing, maybe. Turning dark.

I shivered and shoved the thought away.

We headed down the street, a narrow cobblestone affair that had been built hundreds of years ago. The Vaults had been carved right out of the huge cliff beneath Edinburgh Castle. The old buildings down there were pressed cheek by jowl, each rising about three stories tall. Though they looked like they were built of regular materials, they were actually carved right from the rock itself.

We passed a trio of shops that sold potions, each looking nastier than the last. Bottles full of acid-green liquid lined the window of the first shop, while a massive cauldron bubbled away in the second. The third had windows that were entirely blacked out, and that was scariest of all.

And though it was scary, something in me *liked* it.

Nope. Don't think about it.

There were still a lot of people out and about despite the late hour. Every magical being in the world had a signature—something that hit up one or more of the five senses—and most of the people down here had gross signatures. Dark magic came with disgusting scents, sounds, and tastes. The smell of burning tires or the taste of rotten meat, that kind of thing.

I didn't make eye contact as we slipped by mages and shifters who would spit on us as soon as talk to us. Bree stuck close to me, eyeing everyone suspiciously. They would have no idea how powerful she was, since she suppressed a lot of her signature.

I didn't blame her. Better to fly under the radar. We'd spent most of our childhood running from the Rebel Gods, a fanatical cult that had hunted us because we were Dragon Gods. It'd taught us to be wary and try to blend in with our surroundings.

They'd eventually captured me, keeping me prisoner for five horrible years. But now I was free. I'd lost my gift of telekinesis and had no magic left, but I was free.

Free.

I focused on that, determined not to fall into the darkness.

I skirted around a witch selling fortunes, then hurried toward the back of The Vaults.

"It's quieter back here," Bree said.

"Yeah. Perfect for a murder." I slowed as we neared the bar called Despair, then slipped into an alley nearby. The small cobblestone square was surrounded on all sides by old three-story buildings. Across the square, the shop named Evil stood quiet and empty. Stars sparkled overhead, but they were just an enchantment. There was only rock above us since we were underground, with the castle sitting on top of that.

Bree and I crouched in the alley, sticking to the shadows. The darkness soothed me, which was both weird and probably bad.

"It's here. I can feel it," I whispered.

There was no commotion, no blood, no body. It hadn't happened yet, thank fates. Damned if I'd let the murder actually happen.

Why had I been chosen for this, though? Why would they give *me*—No-Magic Rowan—this clue?

I peered into the darkness, searching each doorway and alley that led off the square. "You see anything? Hear anything?"

"Nothing unusual."

"Good." One of Bree's gifts was enhanced senses. The Norse god Heimdall had given them to her.

Theoretically, there was a Pantheon of gods out there waiting to give me their magic, too, just like they had with Bree and Ana.

But it hadn't happened.

Maybe I wasn't worthy.

Maybe it was the darkness I could feel growing slowly inside me.

Nope. Not going to think about it.

If I didn't think about it, maybe it wasn't real. Maybe I was even imagining it.

A shout sounded from an alley across the way. I stiffened, my fingers tingling where they touched the hilt of the dagger sheathed at my thigh.

Next to me, Bree leaned forward, peering into the dark. "Two people. Young men. Pissed, from the sound of it."

I grinned at the British slang. Pissed equaled drunk. We might live in Scotland now, but our roots were in Death Valley, California. We'd only been in Scotland about six months, but we were already changing to fit it.

At the other side of the small square, the shadows shifted. "See that?"

Bree squinted in that direction. "A man. Big. He's—"

The two drunk men we'd heard stumbled into the alley at that point, cutting her off. They were young. No older than us, and we were only twenty-three. Laughing and joking, they turned toward Despair, their eyes glued to the bright lights in the windows.

Movement from the roofs caught my eye, and I glanced up. Demons jumped down, at least six of them. Each was armed to the teeth, with massive horns spearing the sky. They were a variety of species—all sizes and shapes—and their dark magic rolled off them, stinking of sulfur and death. I didn't recognize any of their species, which meant I wouldn't know what magic they were going to throw at us.

In the sky above, a creature cawed, loud and fierce.

"A bird?" Bree flashed confused eyes toward me.

"What the heck is a bird doing underground?" I looked up, then gasped. It had to be the size of a car. "It's freaking huge."

The massive creature dived, headed for the two men in the middle of the square. It didn't look exactly like a bird. In fact, its image flickered so much it was hard to tell what it was. The demons surrounded the men, but the creature was headed right for them.

Bree looked up. "I've got this."

Magic swirled around her as her silver wings flared from her back. In addition to having the magic of the Norse gods, she was a Valkyrie. It came with some pretty sweet perks. She leapt into the sky, her huge wings carrying her toward the massive winged beast. She drew her sword as she flew.

As awesome as it was to watch Bree fight, I had to stop these demons. There were six of them. Possibly too many for me to fight without magic, but I had my potions.

I drew a potion bomb from the sack at my side, and I hurled it at the nearest demon. It exploded against his back, blue liquid splashing everywhere.

He roared, then fell flat on his face, the paralyzing potion freezing his muscles until he couldn't move.

The two young men stood frozen in the middle as I raced out, sprinting for the demons who were closing in on them. I drew another blue potion bomb—I color coded them according to spell—and hurled it at another demon.

He roared and fell, stiff as a board.

I neared the first demon that I'd paralyzed. He lay face down on the ground, frozen. I drew a sword from the ether, using a bit of handy magic that I'd bought rather than owned myself, and stabbed him in the back of the neck. The cut was quick, and I felt no guilt. Demons were evil, usually taken from hell by black magic and hired to do awful deeds on earth.

I wasn't even technically killing him. When a demon died on earth, their body disappeared and they woke up back in whatever hell they'd come from. Eventually, he'd probably make his way back to earth.

In a way, this was a win-win for both of us. Or at least, not a major loss for the demon.

In the sky, Bree and the giant beast fought, darting around and clashing violently. I looked back to the ground, where *my* fight was happening.

Two of the demons had grabbed the young men and were holding them, but they weren't actually hurting them. I frowned. Were they holding them for the monster that Bree was trying to drive off?

Another demon lunged for me, sword raised. His skin was a pale gray, and he was about six inches taller than me. His horns were a pale white that matched his long fangs and claws. I dived low, narrowly avoiding his steel, my reflexes practiced and quick. I'd worked my ass off at this when I'd realized my magic was gone. If I didn't have power, I'd sure as heck be the fastest, most skilled fighter.

On the ground, I rolled onto my back and popped up onto my feet, swinging my sword for the demon. It sliced toward his middle, but he sucked his stomach in, dodging my blow.

"Lucky bastard." I grinned, darting toward him.

I moved so quickly that his yellow eyes widened in surprise. Then I swiped my blade across his neck. Blood sprayed, and I ducked.

Still, it hit me in the forehead, warm and sticky and gross. I was fast, but not magically fast. Avoiding arterial blood spray was almost impossible. It was one of my least favorite parts of the job.

I kicked the demon in the chest so he fell backward, then whirled to face the fight.

The shadow at the edge of the square moved.

A man stepped out.

Power hit me in the face, magic so strong that I gasped.

And his *face.*

He looked like a fallen angel. One who'd gotten in a brawl as soon as he'd hit earth. Dark hair waved around his face, and his lips were full, his eyes a brilliant blue. His perfect nose was just slightly crooked, as if he'd broken it once or twice. The flaw should have made him look less divine, but somehow, it didn't.

And his body. Holy crap, with those arms, he could break a semitruck in half. He had to be six and a half feet tall, if he was an inch, his shoulders broad and his waist trim.

Time seemed to stop as I looked at him, shrouded in shadow. His magic rolled out from him in waves, complete with every signature in the book. It lit up all five of my senses, something so rare that only a few supernaturals possessed it. It meant he was strong. *Really* strong.

His magic tasted of fine whiskey, burning the back of my throat. It smelled of cedar, fresh and bright, and sounded like the roar of a waterfall. Rarest of all was his aura. Supernaturals almost never had auras, but his was gold, and shaped vaguely like ancient armor, covering him from neck to knees. It shimmered in front of him, there but not, one of the strangest and most fabulous things I'd ever seen.

But strongest of all was the *feel* of his magic. It felt like a caress against my skin. Almost like a kiss. I shivered, trying not to lose myself in the feeling.

This was a fight. One that I wouldn't lose.

I turned away from the man, ignoring the tugging sensation I felt pulling me toward him.

He could be a bad guy—he might be fighting on the side of these demons, after all—but I'd have to deal with him *after* I took out the massive red demon who was bearing down on me like a freight train. The monster was at least seven feet tall, and covered in so much muscle that I wondered how he wiped his own butt.

Ew. Gross. Focus on the fight, Rowan.

The demon's magic smelled of blood and gore and felt like needles piercing my skin. From the feel of his signature, he was as evil as they came. He raised a hand, magic sparking around his massive claws, then hurled a blast of fire at me.

I dived low, feeling the heat streak across my cheek, and drew a potion bomb from my sack. It was bright green, the glass gleaming in the light of the street lamps. I rolled onto my back and hurled the bomb at him just as he threw another fireball.

I scrambled right, taking a hit to my left hip. Pain flared hot and fierce. But the demon shrieked.

Nailed him.

I rolled over to see him flailing, the acid eating its way to his heart. It was a nasty potion bomb, one that I wanted to keep perfecting until it killed more quickly. I didn't like the suffering, even though I used them on demons, who probably ate kids or something horrible like that.

Well, maybe if he was a kid-eater, he should suffer.

I shoved the ridiculous thought away and scrambled to my feet, searching the square. Bree continued to fight off the giant monster, while the two demons held their human captives.

More demons had appeared from the rooftops, but the man from the shadows was taking care of them quickly. As I watched, he strode up to one, not a single weapon in his hand. Was he an elemental mage? Maybe he'd hit him with lightning or something.

But nope.

He got close to the tall gray demon, who swung a wicked-looking sword at him. The man dodged the blade, then reached up and tore the head right off the demon.

"Holy fates!" The words escaped before I realized. He fought like a freaking gladiator.

"I know, right?" The words sounded from out of the blue, but I couldn't see anyone.

What the heck? I looked around, but saw nothing.

Maybe I was imagining them. I was too busy watching the man, anyway. Somehow, he managed to dodge the arterial blood flow. I reached up and touched the demon blood that had now cooled on my forehead.

It was impossible to dodge arterial blood spray. It was too fast.

Not as fast as this guy, though, who clearly had to have some kind of magical speed.

He charged around the square, taking out demon after demon. More appeared, two of them so close to me that I had to turn my attention from the gladiator to fight off the monsters that would kill me as soon as look at me.

I spun to face an oncoming demon. He was too close for a potion bomb—no way I wanted to risk getting hit by the splash—so I raised my sword. "Come and get it, big guy."

He grinned, his yellow fangs making my stomach turn. He'd have breath like dead bodies, I'd bet a crate of double chocolate cookies on it.

He raised his blade, and we clashed, steel against steel. I

dived and parried, narrowly avoiding a slice that could have taken off my leg. He had strength and reach on me, but I had speed. I struck for his sword arm, cutting deep.

He roared and dropped his blade, his green eyes flaring with rage. He raised his other arm, revealing a hand tipped in massive claws, and swiped at me.

I jumped backward, feeling his claws swoosh past my face with only a centimeter to spare. I dodged forward, sinking my sword into his gut.

He gurgled this time, hissing an obscenity that sounded something like "-iserable -unt."

I could only guess where he was going with that, but frankly, I didn't care. Instead, I kicked him in the stomach to dislodge him from my blade and spun to face the fight again, triumph welling within me.

I was too late.

A demon was only feet away, moving so fast that I couldn't get my sword arm up. He grabbed me by the neck, cutting off my air. I gasped, but the air caught in my throat.

Panic swelling in my chest, I raised my sword to strike. He knocked the blade away with his free arm, and the steel clattered to the cobblestones. It was the most terrifying sound I'd ever heard. Losing my weapon while in the grips of a demon. He raised me into the air. I kicked my legs, struggling to break free, and stared death in the face.

2

ACID-GREEN EYES GLARED OUT FROM A PALE-WHITE FACE. SILVER horns reached for the sky, decorated with black scrollwork. His fangs were four inches long, dripping with saliva. And his magic bubbled with evil, feeling like a bath in hot oil. My skin burned fiercely all over.

I reached for the dagger at my thigh, but he grabbed my arm. *Shit.*

I tried with my other hand, but he was unnaturally fast, grabbing that one also so he gripped both in one huge fist.

My lungs burned and my throat ached, feeling like it would be crushed at any moment. Frantic, I searched for Bree. She was still fighting the winged monster, locked in a battle from which she couldn't escape.

The man—the gladiator—was taking out other demons. Not like I could count on him for help anyway.

Fear iced the blood in my veins as panic beat its fists against my ribs, my heart going so fast I thought it would burst.

The demon continued to squeeze, his green eyes studying me.

"You're strange," he said.

So? I wanted to say. Of *course* I was strange to a demon.

And I was about to be dead meat. I felt like a rat caught in a trap, visceral panic streaking through me. Primal and so fierce. I thrashed and kicked, but it did no good.

He could squeeze the life from me any second, but he didn't. It just made my panic worse.

I reached deep for the telekinesis that I'd once possessed. Before my captivity with the Rebel Gods, I'd been able to control any object with my mind alone. Since my escape, I hadn't been able to access it. There was a spark of it deep within me—I could feel it there—but nothing I did allowed me to access it.

It sat low in my belly, dormant. Leaving me to die.

Tears rolled down my cheeks. My lungs were on fire, my limbs turning weak.

I reached for it one last time, desperate to call it to the surface. But I got something else, instead.

Something dark flared to life within me. Not my telekinesis, which was a good magic. A neutral magic.

No, something dark rose up in my belly. Something that suited The Vaults. Something that reminded me of what it felt like to walk down these quiet streets alone and feel at home.

The darkness rose within me, surging through my limbs and my mind. The demon's eyes widened as he stared at me, confusion filling their acid depths.

I was just as confused as he was.

But the magic kept coming, dark and sick. It made my stomach turn as it flowed through me. I swore I could feel it glowing out of my eyes. I might vomit it out any second.

Terror like I'd never known iced through me, far worse than the fear of death at this demon's hands.

There was something wrong with me.

I was full of dark magic.

It wasn't just the tug of enjoyment I felt when I walked in the dark magic district. I was *full* of it.

"You're one of us." Fascination sounded in the demon's voice. "Your soul is ours."

"It's *not*." I wanted to scream the words, but I couldn't even croak them. The magic kept filling me up, ready to burst out of me.

"It will be. The darkness grows, eating you from the inside. I can feel it. Soon, it will devour you." He sounded excited, like he'd never seen anything like it before.

I'm not one of you!

Then it did.

The demon's face lit with a bright light. It had to come from my eyes. I could feel them glowing weirdly. It made no sense, but I could *feel* it.

He gasped and dropped me.

I sucked in a ragged breath, my lungs burning.

But the magic still filled me, dark and sick and horrible. It pushed at my skin, trying to break free. The feeling was so bad I'd take death over this.

I had to get rid of the magic.

Instinct made me raise my hand and grip the demon's throat. His eyes widened, terror glinting in their green depths, and he froze.

Or did *I* freeze him?

I didn't know. All I could do was shove the magic out of me. I pushed it out of my chest, out of my body, forcing it into the demon.

"Don't do this," he begged. "You're one of us."

"I'm not." My heart thundered. The dark magic poured from me, flowing into the demon. It made my head spin.

His skin turned gray, darker and darker, and the acid light left his eyes.

"Soon." The word whispered past his lips. Then he turned to dust, crumbling at my feet.

I gasped and stepped back, horror welling within me.

How had I done that?

What was that?

Mind roaring, I looked up.

And met the gladiator's eyes. Shock gleamed in their blue depths. Shock and suspicion. Around him, the bodies of demons lay. He'd killed almost every one.

The two remaining demons who held the young men captive took one look at me, their faces paling. Then they dropped their captives and ran, sprinting into the darkness of the alley behind him.

The gladiator gave me a look, then he stared after the demons, clearly unsure of who to chase.

Wait, was *I* a bad guy now?

Would that gladiator hunt *me*?

Just as the terrifying thought streaked through my mind, Bree landed in front of me, covered in blood, eyes wild.

"We've got to get out of here." Her words snapped out, a whip.

I glanced at the sky. The winged monster was gone.

Before I could look back at her, I felt her strong grip on my wrist. She tugged, sprinting down the alley and dragging me with her. I gave the gladiator one last look, then ran for it, racing behind Bree.

She was right.

Whatever had happened there, it was *bad* news.

I was full of dark magic, and the gladiator had seen. He was clearly fighting on the side of right if he was killing the demons. If he worked for the Order of the Magica—the magical government that oversaw all magic users like mages and witches and warlocks—he could report me.

I would be thrown in the Prison for Magical Miscreants if anyone knew I had a power like this. It was pure evil.

My heart thundered as I sprinted away from the scene of the crime. I caught sight of three small shadows against the wall—some kind of small animals, I thought—but they were gone in a flash. Bree and I raced down the darkened cobblestones, turning right onto the main street and downhill toward the exit of The Vaults. We had to get back to the Grassmarket and get to the portal that led to the Protectorate castle.

Only there would I be safe.

But would they accept me back if they knew what I was becoming?

I'd felt something dark inside me ever since I'd come back from my captivity. Had it been this? Had I brought it with me?

Soon.

The demon's last word echoed in my mind. I'd become one of them soon, my soul devoured.

Holy fates, that sounded bad.

"Almost there," Bree panted.

"You could fly, you know." The words cost me what little breath I had, and I nearly stumbled.

She huffed a laugh. "As if I'd leave you."

Warmth filled me, just a spark to provide light in the darkness of what my soul was becoming.

We passed bars and shops, dark magic spilling from them. Not all were evil, but all definitely walked the line with the law. Mr. Amos waved at me from the window of his pygmy toad shop as we raced by, sprinting for the exit.

We ran out, entering the enchanted bookshop that acted as the secret entryway.

"Don't knock anything over!" the house shrieked as we hurried through the shelves stuffed full of books.

No one actually lived or worked here—the house itself was enchanted to dissuade people from entering The Vaults—but I never wanted to piss it off.

The night was cool and dark as we exited the enchanted bookshop, spilling out onto the end of the main street in the Grassmarket. This was where all the regular, not-evil supernaturals in Edinburgh lived and worked. It didn't stink of dark magic or feel like spiders crawling across my skin, so it was a major upgrade compared to The Vaults. Old, three-story buildings lined the cobblestone street and housed bars and restaurants, along with a few shops. Apartments sat on the top floors.

The sound of bagpipes drifted toward us from somewhere far away, and the shouts of revelers in the pubs spilled out of open doors. Spring was coming, and even supernaturals were happy to welcome the warmer temperatures.

"What the hell was that?" Bree demanded as we hurried down the street, desperate to reach the portal that would take us straight back to the Protectorate castle.

"I don't know." I could barely catch my breath, a combination of exertion and fear.

"Let's just get back." She turned down the alley where the portal was located, and stepped right into the glowing blue hole in the ether. Only Protectorate members could see it and enter it, and I was grateful every time that I stepped in and the ether sucked me through space, taking me home.

I followed her, praying that it would work this time, that I wasn't so evil that it would evict me.

I wasn't, right?

Thankfully, the ether sucked me in as normal, but I swore it felt the tiniest bit strange. Like it didn't want to, at first.

We arrived in the enchanted glen in silence. The Protectorate castle was located on the far north coast of Scotland, a massive structure surrounded by a huge wall. Within the wall was an old fae forest where the magic made it possible to have portals to the outside world.

Bree led the way through the twisted old trees. Fairy lights floated on the air, twinkling between the branches and tree trunks. By the time we exited the forest and reached the main castle lawn, tension thrummed across my skin.

A half moon shined on the huge castle that sat in the middle of the grounds. Towers and turrets speared toward the sky as the mullioned glass sparkled in the darkness. I'd only lived there for six months, but I loved it like my forever home. Who wouldn't?

But if the Protectorate leaders found out that I now possessed such dark magic? They might evict me.

As if she didn't want to speak of my new magic out in the open, Bree hurried across the castle grounds in silence. We crossed the rolling hills and approached the huge castle. The large wooden doors swung open to admit us entrance, and we climbed the steps to the entry hall. Two huge sweeping staircases led up to the second floor, and we took the steps two at a time.

Each of us had a tower apartment at the back of the castle.

"Let's go to mine," I said.

She nodded.

We hurried down the hall and reached the door that led to my tower. My touch unlocked it, and we climbed the stairs. We were halfway up when a third set of footsteps sounded from below.

"Ana?" I called. My third sister was the only other one besides Bree who was allowed to unlock the door to my space.

"Yeah. What happened? You guys took forever."

"Come on up." I hurried up the last few steps to the main apartment and let myself in.

When I'd first moved in, the place had looked like any other normal apartment. Now, it looked like a mad scientist's laboratory. When I'd been rescued from the Rebel Gods captivity and hadn't had any magic left, I'd needed *something*. First, I'd learned to fight, and then I'd learned to make potion bombs. My friend Connor from Magic's Bend, an all-magic city in Oregon, had taught me most of the potions. Bree's boyfriend, Lachlan, was also a potion's master, so he'd helped, too. The others I'd picked up from research in the library.

I'd dedicated every waking hour to mastering potions. Humans couldn't make potions—you needed at least a little magic in you. And I had that. It was inaccessible to me, but it was enough that I could manage to make most of what I needed.

"Whoa, there's even more stuff in here than there was last week," Bree said.

I eyed the new setup at the far edge of the round tower room. The table was covered with a complex contraption meant to distill the essence of magical plants. Connor had helped me build it.

Worry shadowed Bree's eyes. "Don't you think you might be going a bit overboard with the potions? There isn't even a couch in here anymore."

I frowned at her. "I have no magic, Bree. I need *something*."

Bree pursed her lips. "That's not exactly true anymore."

"Not true anymore?" Ana's voice sounded from the door. "What do you mean? Did Rowan get some magic?"

I turned to look at my second sister. She was about my height—thoroughly average—but with blonde hair instead of brown and bright green eyes.

"I don't know what I got," I said. "But it's not good."

I'd been keeping this little secret for months now—the knowledge that something darker was growing inside me. My affinity for The Vaults had become even stronger lately, and considering that I'd just destroyed a demon with black magic, it was time for me to come clean.

I swallowed hard at the thought.

"What happened when you guys left?" Ana asked. "Something's up, isn't it?"

Bree leaned against a table and looked at me. I hadn't had a chance yet to tell Ana about the notes that sent me on vigilante missions, but that was only because she'd been busy with her work for the Protectorate. I couldn't avoid it any longer.

"I've taken up some extracurricular activities." I explained the notes and the missions I'd been going on, ending with the one tonight. I described the young men and the demons, but omitted my weird new magic and the handsome gladiator man. My gaze turned to Bree. "But what the hell was that creature?"

"You said it was huge. And in The Vaults?" Ana sounded appropriately incredulous.

"Totally huge," Bree said. "It looked a bit like an owl, but the image would flicker and then it'd look like a person. Then like a monster. I have no idea what species it was, but it was bigger than me. I've never seen anything like it."

"All that blood is from superficial wounds, right?" Ana asked. "I mean, I figure they are since you're standing. But doesn't hurt to ask."

"Minor stuff." Bree grimaced. "But that monster had some sharp claws."

"It seemed like the demons were there to capture the two men and hold them until the monster could get to them," I said.

"Agreed." Bree nodded. "They grabbed the victims early on but didn't hurt them. And that beast wouldn't stop diving for them."

"Giant monster attacks." Ana frowned. "Not ideal."

"Weird as hell." But not as weird as my new dark magic. I

met Bree's eyes, and she was clearly thinking the same thing. "Something else happened."

Ana turned curious eyes toward me. "This is about your magic?"

"Yeah, and it's dark. Really dark. I disintegrated a demon."

Ana's brows jumped. "Disintegrated?"

"Yeah. I've been feeling a pull toward The Vaults lately. Something in me likes the dark magic. But today, it burst out of me, and I destroyed a demon. Turned him right into dust."

The memory made me shudder.

"That's not the telekinesis magic you were born with, though," Ana said. "Do you think you're getting your Dragon God powers? Did you hear any voices giving you instructions when the power rose inside you?"

"No." I shook my head.

Both she and Bree had gone through the transition to Dragon God. According to them, new powers would appear, along with a disembodied voice that gave vague instructions on how to use them.

"I don't think this is the Dragon God magic. It's so dark. Neither of you have magic this dark."

"Do you think it's a holdover from your time in captivity with the Rebel Gods?" Bree asked.

As much as I hated the idea that there was anything left in me from my time with those monsters, it was the most logical thing. "It could be. The demon said I was like him."

"Demon touched?" Bree asked.

I swallowed hard, nodding. "Possibly."

The Rebel Gods had stolen my telekinesis and given me some of their power in return, so I could do their bidding. I'd thought it was all gone, but apparently not.

"The demon said it would devour my soul until I was like them."

Ana and Bree paled.

"When?" Ana croaked the word.

"Soon."

"What the hell does that even mean?" Bree asked.

"I don't know." But not knowing was eating me up inside.

Ana frowned, then strode to the big wooden chest that crouched in the corner.

I stepped forward, hands outstretched. "No, Ana. I don't want to."

"I don't care." She knelt at the chest and opened it, then withdrew a rock.

I cringed backward.

She turned and held it up. "Just try, Rowan. Please. Your magic is in here."

"It's not." When the Rebel Gods had stolen my telekinesis—essentially, my magical soul—my sisters had tried to get it back. They'd put it in this damned rock and were convinced that I could just take it back. "I've told you it's not that simple. There's evil in that rock along with my magic. The Rebel Gods polluted it."

As long as I had a spark of the telekinesis deep inside me—which I did—I wasn't going to risk taking the polluted magic from the rock. I already had enough darkness in me.

"There might be evil inside you now, too," Bree said.

I flinched. "There *is* evil inside me."

It was devouring my *soul.*

"We have to find a way to get rid of it," she continued.

"I know." Again, I shuddered. It'd been good to save myself from the demon, but the *way* I'd done it? No thanks.

"That's not our only problem," Bree said. "That man saw you."

The memory of him made me warm and cold at the same time. I flushed. Damn it. I was a freaking adult, and that was teenager shit. I really needed to be focusing on the cold—the fear would keep me alive.

Ana's eagle eyes darted from Rowan to me. "What man?"

"Some big strong gladiator-looking dude," I said. "He was clearly a good guy. He took out the demons like they were made of paper, tearing off heads left and right. He was there to save the guys who were under attack."

"And he saw Rowan use her new disintegration magic." Bree's eyes darkened. "There's no way he missed your new magical signature."

Panic flared in my chest, and my eyes darted to her. "What do you mean?"

"When you disintegrated the demon, your magic smelled like decay."

Horror opened a hole in my chest. "I have a new magical signature?"

Bree nodded. "Dark, to go with your new dark magic."

Shit. Shit. Shit. "That means there is no way this is the Dragon God magic. That's never evil. This is something new. And worse."

"We'll get to the bottom of it," Bree said. "I swear."

"We'll do whatever we can to help." Ana turned and put the rock back in the chest, then shut the lid.

A bit of tension seeped from my muscles as I watched my own personal albatross go back into hiding. I couldn't let go of the rock because it had my magic in it. But I also couldn't try to get the magic out because I could feel how tainted it was. The Rebel Gods had screwed it up, and no way would I be messing with it. I had enough problems without inviting them back into my life. They'd kept my mind poisoned for years so I'd be a docile captive. I was finally free, and I was going to stay that way.

I'd started the morning with one problem—stop the murder. Now I was ending it with several. I needed to keep the gladiator quiet. I needed to figure out which demons were freaking *murdering* people with their giant monster pet. And I needed to get rid of the dark magic that was going to devour my soul. Oh, and I needed to figure out how to hide the darkness until I could get rid of it.

Damn, that was a lot to do.

3

THE NEXT MORNING, A POUNDING SOUNDED ON MY DOOR, followed by tromping footsteps coming up my stairs.

I popped upright from my crappy little bed on the floor and scrambled to my feet. I scrubbed my eyes, then stumbled down the metal spiral stairs.

Ana stood in the middle of my living room, grinning. "Morning!"

"It's too early to be so cheerful." I yawned hard.

She smiled even bigger and shoved a coffee mug at me. "I thought you might want this."

I stared down at it. "You didn't make it, right?"

She laughed. "Course not. I actually like you. No way I'm going to kill you with my coffee."

"Good." I sipped the coffee. It warmed my belly at the same time her gesture warmed my heart.

She shoved her way into my crowded little apartment. Muffin, her hairless cat, flew in after her. The battered looking old tom had gotten wings a few months ago and now preferred to fly everywhere. He greeted me with a low meow, his emerald earring glinting in the light.

I grinned at him. "Hey, Muffin."

"You really do need to clear some of this out and make room for a coffee machine at least," Ana said. "You don't suck at making it."

"No need." I weaved toward the little open spot on the table to sit. "I can always get it from Hans. Just like you do."

Hans was the castle cook. His kitchen was located under the entry hall and was the perfect place to pop in and grab a bite.

"That's not really the point." Ana's gaze traveled around the apartment. "This place is getting a bit nuts."

"Ah." I put down the coffee. "So this comes with a lecture. Didn't do enough of that last night?"

"I'm just worried about you, is all. It's been tough adjusting. I know that."

"I'm fine."

"And you're going to class?"

I scowled at her. I'd wanted to skip to spend time figuring out what the heck was wrong with me, but now I realized what the deal was. She was here to drag me to class, not just to deliver coffee. "Of course I'm going."

I wasn't sure if I meant it, but I wanted to get her off my case.

"Good. You might not have magic, but you're the best with weapons that the Protectorate has ever seen. You've got mad skills, Rowan. You deserve to be here as much as anyone else. It's your first official day, and you need to stake your claim."

My eyes prickled with tears. Leave it to my sister to see right into the heart of the issue and stab it with her dagger-like intellect.

"Thanks." I looked to the side. "But I need to get to the library and try to find out what the hell is going wrong with me."

"Bree's already on it. She's got the morning off, so she's hunting for answers."

I had the best sisters in the world. "I'll join her after class, then." I jumped off the table. "But I've got to grab a shower if I'm going to make it in time. Thanks for the coffee."

"Anytime." She gave me one last look. "I'm off to figure out who is releasing Lockert demons from their hell. I'll meet you when I'm done."

"Thanks. And be careful."

Ana had just graduated from the Protectorate Academy a few months ago. In record time, just like Bree. She was now a member of the PITs, the Paranormal Investigative Team. It came with jobs like saving important people and solving mysteries.

Really cool, actually. Definitely a top job at the Protectorate, and one I wouldn't hate having myself, if I could ever graduate.

Ana left, and I swung into the kitchen to grab some double chocolate cookies for breakfast. Bree might give me crap for such an unhealthy start to the day, but I didn't care. After years in captivity, I was going to eat whatever the heck I wanted. More often than not, it was double chocolate cookies.

I ate them quickly as I climbed the stairs to my bedroom, then grabbed a quick shower. All cleaned up, I selected an outfit for the day. As usual, it was tight black jeans covered in holes, a hot pink T-shirt with an obscure band logo from my friend Connor, and a black leather jacket that matched my boots. For a while I'd been wearing all black, but as I got used to life outside of captivity—and became less worried about lying low, since all the Rebel Gods were dead—I'd started bringing a lot of pink into my wardrobe. Hot pink, normally.

I pulled my hair up into a messy knot and slicked on some pink lipstick. A spell would keep it from wearing off during the day. Potions came in handy for things like that, and people rarely saw the hit coming if you were wearing lipstick called Pink Power.

As the last—and most important—part of my preparations, I packed my miniature emergency kit. Carefully, I slipped tiny vials of different potions into a specially sewn black leather belt. The vials were so tiny that they hid fully beneath the belt's leather. I never knew what I'd need, but these were the basics. Tracking, healing, divining—over a dozen different highly concentrated potions that I'd worked hard to develop over the last six months. I had a knack for it, fortunately.

Ready to face class, I hurried out of my apartment. The castle was quiet this early in the morning, with most people still in their apartments. I passed a couple of sleepy demon hunters. I didn't know their names, but I'd seen them hanging around with Jesse Ammons, the leader of the demon hunters unit.

As I neared the huge room at the back of the castle that was used for Academy training sessions, my heart picked up speed just the tiniest bit. I tugged on my jacket, ignoring the nerves, and stepped into the huge room.

Jude, the trainer for today, stood at the far side of the room. Her dark skin gleamed under the light, and her braids fell halfway down her back. She was the head of the PITs, Ana's division, and sometimes she took over training at the Academy.

Jude looked at me, her pale blue eyes full of sparkles that looked like stars. She had the most amazing eyes I'd ever seen—eyes that could see everything, it seemed.

Please don't see my weird new magic.

I did my best to pull it tight to my chest. I wasn't used to controlling my magical signature, but I was going to have to learn if I didn't want to get thrown in the Prison for Magical Miscreants.

"Great. Glad you're here, Rowan." She turned back to the other Academy members, and I noticed them for the first time. "Rowan is officially starting with us today."

There were only four in the class, all in their early twenties like me, and they murmured hello. It was a bit like a magical version of the FBI Academy.

I looked toward the students. Lavender stood with Angus. They'd been at the Academy when my sisters were going through a few months ago. Of course my sisters had graduated in record time and left these two behind, which made them hate Ana and Bree. They hated me, too, but I kind of liked the enmity. Distracted me from my nerves.

Lavender turned to glare at me, her dark hair flowing around her shoulders.

I grinned widely at her and waved. I might not *feel* like I belonged here, but I sure as hell could fake it pretty damned well. As long as it meant annoying Lavender.

Two other students turned to look curiously at me, but I didn't pay them any attention. I thought they were called Carl and Lorence, but I wasn't sure.

Jude gave me a studying look, one that made my skin itch. It felt like she could see right into me. Could she see the strange dark magic that was lurking in my soul?

"All right," Jude said. "Since this is Rowan's first day, we're going to do a training exercise. Figure out where everyone is with their combat skills. And we have a new instructor to help with that." She looked at her wrist, her brow furrowed. "He should be here any moment."

Jude looked up toward the door, and her smile widened.

He was here.

I couldn't hear him approach, but I could feel it.

Hot and cold raced across my skin as I turned. That whiskey taste and cedar scent...

Time slowed again as I spotted him, striding in through the door.

The gladiator from last night.

Holy crap, he was here.

And he'd seen my evil magic.

I wanted to run. My gaze darted around, but there was no

reasonable escape. I tried to calm my breathing. There was no guarantee that he would mention what he'd seen to Jude. And if he did, there was no guarantee that she'd kick me out of the Protectorate.

I drew in a steadying breath.

I'd spent five years as a captive to evil gods. I'd learned how to suck it up and keep going, and that's what I was going to do.

Just before I dragged my gaze away from him, he looked at me.

Recognition flashed in his eyes. Then something else.

Heat?

An impossibly small smile quirked at the side of his mouth, but was quickly gone.

I frowned. Did I imagine that?

Then his gaze hardened, and I *knew* I wasn't imagining that.

Yep, this guy was wondering what the hell I was. Join the club, buddy. I had no freaking idea, either.

He strode over to join Jude, his powerful legs eating up the ground. For such a big man, he moved with leonine grace.

Next to me, Lavender whispered something to Angus. Whatever it was, the kid blushed.

If she was saying that the gladiator was totally hot, I had to agree. I didn't want to agree, but it was like saying the sky was blue. It was just a fact.

He stopped next to Jude and folded his hands over each other in a relaxed waiting position. His gaze swept over the crowd of students. There were only five of us, so it didn't take long.

When his gaze landed on me, it lingered. I scowled at him, determined to keep the blush at bay. It probably wasn't the smartest move, given that I wanted to fly under the radar, but he got my back up.

Jude shot him a glance, then turned her gaze to the crowd.

"This is Maximus Valerius. He's here to help us with our fighting skills."

Maximus.

I'd called him a gladiator in jest, but maybe I wasn't that far off.

A murmur rolled through the crowd, as if they recognized the name. I sure didn't. He was powerful enough to be famous, but I didn't know for what.

Unfortunately, Jude didn't provide any more explanations. And Maximus seemed to be the strong, silent type. If I wanted to know more, I'd probably have to ask Lavender, who seemed to recognize his name.

No way in hell.

"We'll start with a fighting exercise to examine your strengths and weakness," Jude said. "You're all welcome to use your magic." Her gaze turned to me. "Or not, as the case may be."

I shifted, slightly uncomfortable at being called out. But whatever. I was used to it.

Maximus waved his strong arm, and magic sparked on the air, smelling of cedar and sounding like a crashing waterfall.

In the middle of the massive room, the air began to shimmer. Objects appeared, huge towers and low boulders. A dozen of them soon dotted the space, providing cover for our fight.

Damn, he was powerful. Conjurers could create things out of thin air, but creating stuff this big? That took a *lot* of power. What the heck was he, besides a conjurer and general badass?

As he worked, conjuring more objects, Jude approached. She had a bag in her hand, along with a short, blunt sword. She held them out to me. "Since you don't fight with your magic, I thought you could use these."

I took the sword, the use of which was obvious, but had to

dig into the bag to figure out what was inside. My hand closed around a smooth glass sphere, and I pulled it out.

"Meant to simulate one of your potion bombs," she said. "Filled with a temporary sedative. It won't put your target to sleep, but it should weaken them enough that they can't walk well. You can finish them off with the sword."

I grinned at her. "I can work with this."

"I thought so." Her gaze turned briefly to Maximus, who was still working on creating the setting for the fight to come. "We've brought Maximus here specifically for you, Rowan. If you aren't able to access your magic, your fight skills will need to be unparalleled if you want to pass the Academy and join the Protectorate."

"I do want that." It would secure my place here, allowing me to join my sisters in the ranks of the Protectorate staff. It was a position I wanted desperately. Not just for the security, but because I liked the idea of helping people. I'd been helpless for so much of my life; I wanted to turn the tables and be the one in control. The one making things better.

"Good." She nodded. "Then try hard today. It was difficult to get Maximus to agree to come here for training. It's not his usual. You'll need to impress him to get him to train you."

I swallowed hard, really not liking the sound of this. One, he was hot and I was shallow, so it was hard to focus around him. Two—and much worse—he'd seen my new dark magic. *This* was the guy I was supposed to convince to help make me *more* dangerous?

Sounded like a tall order.

Jude turned and left. Maximus was done creating the layout for our faux battle, and he and Jude were talking in low voices. My competitors were splitting up to find hiding spaces, and I needed to join them.

I slung the bag of potions over my back and hiked it toward

high ground, climbing onto one of the towers in the middle of the space. From there, I could spot a half dozen large rocks that provided shelter, along with four other similar towers. Fake trees provided more cover, and through the branches of one, I could spot Angus's red hair.

Target number one, sighted.

I crouched low, concealing as much of my form as I could. Tension thrummed in the air as we waited for the fight to start. My gaze darted toward the gladiator.

His eyes were right on me.

A shiver raced down my spine, and I looked away.

"Ready." Maximus's deep voice cut through the room. It was the first time I'd heard him speak, and woo boy, did he sound like sex on a stick. *No. Bad, Rowan.* "Set. Go!"

As if a switch had been flicked, I launched into fight mode, jumping up and hurling my potion bomb at Angus. All the practice paid off, because the blue glass ball flew through the air, slipping between the fake tree branches and slamming into Angus's back.

Moron.

I leapt down from the top of the tower and landed in a crouch. I'd spent the last six months acting like some parkour nerd, leaping off ledges and learning to move quickly through impossible scenarios.

This was cake.

I raced toward Angus, my sword gripped in my hand, and found him lying facedown at the base of the tree, his head turned slightly so that he could glare at me.

I tapped the tip of my sword to the back of his neck. "Gotcha."

"Bitch," he managed to hiss.

"Right on the first try." I grinned, then spun and sprinted away.

Sure, I was never going to make friends if I kept behaving like this, but I already had my sisters.

Something flashed out of the corner of my eye. A large rock was flying right toward me.

Shit!

I dived low, barely avoiding the stone as it flew overhead and slammed into the castle wall. The whole room shook, and I scowled.

Seriously? Jude gave me a fake sword and potion bombs when Lavender was allowed to use her telekinesis with such deadly force?

Not fair.

And I was jealous. I believed in intellectual honesty, and sure as shit I was jealous of Lavender's telekinesis. That used to be *my* power.

I shoved away the useless emotions and scrambled to my feet, whirling to find her.

Boulders, fake trees, and wooden towers blocked my view. Not a single glimpse of that jerk. Quickly, I darted behind a rock, making sure it was a big one. Too big for Lavender to pick up with her magic, at least.

I took a moment to catch my breath, then peeked out from behind the rock.

Where the hell was she?

And where were the others?

All was silent out there.

If Lavender was stalking me, the other two should be fighting, right?

But I heard no sound of combat. Smelled and tasted no flaring magic.

Quiet footsteps sounded from far off on the left. The right, as well. I had good hearing, thankfully. Nothing like Bree's, but good.

And right now, it indicated one thing.

They were ganging up on me.

My skin chilled.

This was fake combat, but still. It made me nervous. I felt like prey.

Anger surged warm under my skin, driving away the fear. I *hated* being afraid. I'd spent five years being afraid. That was enough for me.

They wanted to gang up on me?

Fine.

They wouldn't like the results.

Slowly, I sucked in a calming breath, reaching with my hearing to try to locate my stalkers. I searched the area behind me, briefly catching on Maximus. He watched me, his gaze steady.

I wanted to give him a show. No way I was going to let these jerks get the upper hand on me.

My senses revealed that two opponents were closing in on me in a pincer-like movement. I couldn't hear the third—who I'd bet big money was Lavender. If it *was* her, she'd be up high, wanting a good vantage point from which to use her telekinesis. It was what I would have done.

Once I had a bead on the two who were closing in, I drew a potion bomb from my pouch. Ready, I scrambled on top of the rock, my gaze going right. It landed on Carl, the dark-haired guy with fire magic. His startled gaze met mine just as I hurled my potion bomb.

He was quick, throwing his blast of fire before my bomb collided with his chest. I leapt off the rock, rolling on the ground to hide behind a tree trunk. Carl shouted as the potion bomb slammed into him, and I heard him hit the ground.

One down, two to go.

I still had a pretty good idea where the other attacker was. To the left, about ten yards away. Probably hiding. Wimp.

I grabbed another potion bomb and lunged out from behind the tree. Magic flared on the air, and I looked up just in time to see a rock the size of a football flying toward me. In the distance, I caught sight of Lavender's dark hair.

Jerk.

I dived right, avoiding the rock as it plowed into the tree. Another followed soon after, and it was clear that Lavender was going to throw everything she had at me.

I played a game of Frogger, sprinting across the fake forest as Lavender threw rocks at me. When a spear of ice flew from between the leaves of a large fake bush, I knew exactly where the other fighter was hiding.

Hiding. *As if* that would work.

"Just freaking hold still!" Frustration sounded in Lavender's voice.

I stifled a laugh. That would definitely get points docked off. Deadly and silent, that was the way to be.

I dodged another icicle and finally caught sight of a pair of eyes peering out from between the branches. Then they darted away. He was running. I pursued, following Lorence to the left. Just as he darted out from behind the bush, I hurled my potion bomb.

It exploded against his side, and he went down in a tumble of limbs. I sprinted toward him, tapping him with my sword, then whirled to find Carl. He should still be down, and the kill wouldn't count if I didn't tap him with my sword and take him out.

Lavender hurled rocks at me as I ran through the fake forest. I'd take out Carl, then I'd finish with her.

One of the small boulders whizzed past my face as I neared a tree, and I realized I was getting sloppy. I spared Lavender another glance, just in time to see a second rock head straight for me. I spun out of the way, taking an indirect hit to the shoulder.

Pain flared, but I ignored it.

Lavender crowed in delight, and it was almost impossible for me to ignore *that.*

Instead of heading for her, I sprinted the last few feet toward Carl, who was struggling to sit. Whatever freezing potion Jude had put in these bombs, it wasn't lasting long.

I tapped my blade to his throat, and he glared at me.

I indulged myself with a smirk, then turned to go after Lavender.

There were no more rocks flying at me.

That was trouble.

She was getting smarter.

Warily, I searched my surroundings as I raced on silent feet toward her. When the tree to my right began to creak and lean toward me, my heart leapt.

Crap!

The tree picked up speed, falling in my direction.

I dived forward and skidded on the ground as the tree slammed down behind me. A quick glance up showed Lavender leaning over the railing on her tower, her eyes bright on mine.

"Is that all you got?" I asked, unable to help myself. There was no need to be silent anymore. My target knew where I was.

She scowled and raised her hands, magic flaring.

Okay, time to end this. Playing with my prey wasn't smart.

I surged to my feet and sprinted toward her, wanting to finish hand to hand. The tower that she stood upon was about twenty feet tall, mostly smooth sided except for a series of protruding boards. They were like little notches, perfect for climbing. There should be stairs around the back, if it were like all the other towers in the room, but I didn't have time for that.

I leapt toward the notches on the side of the tower, using them to scale the thing as quickly as I could. Lavender's startled eyes met mine, and I pushed myself harder. I leapt over the railing just as she made a massive boulder levitate near my head.

She was going for a kill shot. This was bullshit.

I ducked beneath the rock, feeling the thing skim the top of my head and probably take out a few hairs. Then I swung my sword, tapping her on the side of the neck.

"Dead." I nearly snarled the words.

She hissed at me. An honest to fates *hiss.*

In the distance, my gaze caught on Maximus. His appraising expression ignited my curiosity, but I had to deal with Lavender first. Except I didn't have time for a response.

"Attack!" a familiar voice called from behind.

I turned.

Florian Bumbledomber, the ghostly night librarian, stood in the doorway, his nearly transparent eyes wild. As usual, he wore an old-timey outfit that featured lots of ruffles and brocade. The tall, curly wig on his head was slightly askew, and next to him flew Mayhem, the ghostly pug with wings. Mayhem was Bree's sidekick, but she often spent time in the library.

Jude strode toward Florian, her starry blue eyes suddenly serious. "What kind of attack?"

"In the Grassmarket. A murder, out in plain sight, right in front of the Whiskey and Warlock. Ali and Haris just delivered the news."

"Who was killed?" Maximus's voice cracked like a whip from the back of the room.

"I don't know." Florian twisted his ghostly hands. "The body was mauled beyond recognition. They're requesting the investigative team."

Mauled? What the hell? The Grassmarket was in the *city.*

Mauled was the word you used when a bear got to you. Or some other giant animal. Not a city murder.

The memory of the giant monster flashed in my mind.

Could it be?

Jude didn't waste time turning to look at us. "Class is over."

With that, she strode out, her dark braids bouncing. I turned to find Maximus, but he was already gone, too. I hadn't even seen him leave.

Without sparing a glance at Lavender, I scrambled down the tower and sprinted out of the room.

If the winged monster was back, that meant the demons might be, too. The demon who said I was like them.

This was obviously somehow connected to what was happening to me.

More importantly, *I'd failed.*

There had been a murder, and I'd missed it. We might have foiled it last night, but they'd come back.

I had to find out what the hell was going on.

4

I FOLLOWED JUDE AT A DISCRETE DISTANCE, HURRYING THROUGH the halls of the Protectorate. I'd practiced moving silently, and it was paying off. She didn't look back once.

I couldn't see Maximus, however. Wherever he'd gone, he'd gotten there in a hurry.

Jude made quick work, cutting through the wide, stone hallways of the castle and across the lawn. I tucked myself into a nook in the exterior of the castle until she moved into the forest, then I darted across the lawn after her.

Despite the bright morning sun that hovered in the sky, the forest was dark. The gnarled old trees cut out the light until the only illumination was provided by the fairy lights that fluttered in the air.

By the time I reached the clearing where the portals were situated, Jude had already disappeared through the one leading to Edinburgh. There were three portals in the forest, or at least, there *had* been three. The one leading to the faerie realm was now dead and closed, a mere shadow of itself. The other two portals glowed healthily, though. The blue one led to Edinburgh, and the white to Magic's Bend, Oregon, a large supernatural city where a few of my friends lived.

I slipped through the portal, feeling the ether grab me and suck me through space. My head spun briefly, then I was spit out in the darkened alley in the Grassmarket.

I snuck out onto the street, keeping close to the buildings and hiding behind the crowd of people on the sidewalk. Murder drew a crowd, which was no surprise. The place was teeming with supernaturals who wanted a better look. It was easy to keep myself hidden amongst such a large group.

I slipped through the people, seeking the scene of the crime.

When I came upon it, my stomach turned.

Two men lay on the ground in front of the Whiskey and Warlock, my favorite pub. They were different men from last night, and not nearly as lucky. Their intestines were spilled on the ground around them. For all the fighting I'd done in my life, I couldn't quite remember seeing intestines outside of someone's body.

I swallowed hard and studied the scene, my skin chilling.

This was the work of that giant monster. It had to be. It might have even eaten part of the men, but it was hard to tell.

No weapon did damage like that. It was too rough, too aggressive. Swords could do serious damage. So could magic. But this really looked like a beast had gotten the men with its giant beak or claws.

Which meant that the demons had probably been here, too. What were they doing with this giant monster? Training it to kill?

My gaze scanned the crowd, hoping to find one, though I knew it was unlikely.

Jude was leading part of the investigative team in setting up the scene. Caro, the water mage, was stringing a rope around the site, her short platinum hair bright and messy. Ali and Haris, the djinn twins, were searching for clues, their eyes keen on the ground around the bodies. Their dark hair gleamed in the sunlight. Caro, Ali, and Haris were three of my favorite people at the Protectorate.

Bree and Ana were the last two members of the team, but Ana was off on a mission and Bree was probably still in the library, hunting for clues about my new problem and unaware of the murder.

Though I couldn't see the gladiator, I could feel him somewhere in the crowd. His magic was too strong to miss.

Near the bodies, Ali had picked up a feather off the ground and was studying it.

A clue, definitely. There was nothing else near the bodies.

I scanned the rest of the space, my gaze finally landing on a raccoon sitting on top of a dumpster. They weren't even native to Scotland, were they? He fiddled with something in his little hands.

Another feather?

My heart thudded.

A damned big feather, just like the one Ali held. Most of it was lying on top of the dumpster, but that was *definitely* a giant feather.

I sidled closer to the alley, cutting between a shifter and a witch, then behind a vampire whose fangs made me shiver. His eyes were bright and his fangs long—he *clearly* liked the sight of all this blood.

"Get a hold of yourself, dude," I muttered.

I didn't wait around for his response, slipping up beside the animal who was mostly hidden in shadow. No one had noticed him yet, since they were so focused on the crime scene, but they'd turn this way eventually. Ali was still studying his feather.

The raccoon's feather was identical, and I wanted it.

I eyed him, and he eyed me back, his dark eyes bright within his black mask. Little fingers continued to fiddle with his prize.

Slowly, I reached for it.

He yanked it away. *What the hell do you think you're doing?*

My jaw dropped. I stared at him, dumbfounded. "You can talk?"

Of course I can talk, nitwit.

I glanced around to see if anyone else was noticing, but no one paid me any mind. We were tucked out of the way in the alley, and no one over here was spilling their guts. Literally. That made us boring, despite the talking raccoon.

Ooookay then. "Well, can I have that feather?"

His eyes turned cunning. *What will you give me for it?*

"Trash? Raccoons love trash, right?"

I'd like to say that's a stereotype, but I do love trash.

"Then my trash is your trash."

Allll *your trash?*

"Sure."

You've got a deal.

Well, that was easy. I wasn't sure how he was going to collect on the promise of all my garbage, but that was their problem.

I held out my hand, and the raccoon handed over the feather.

My fingertips closed around it, and a shudder of discomfort raced up my arm. Not only did the feather have an uncomfortable physical signature, the stink of dark magic surrounded it, impossible to ignore.

I reached for my belt and slipped out a tiny vial of potion.

What's that?

"Psychometros potion. My pride and joy." I focused on twisting off the little top and pouring a single drop of the potion onto the feather. It glittered brightly, a silver hue that soaked into the feather.

What's it do?

"Helps me read this object's history." I raised the feather to my lips and touched my tongue to the silver sheen, wincing at the grossness of licking this random monster feather.

Ew. I eat trash, and even that is gross.

"I know." But it worked. The potion fizzed on my tongue, and a vision flashed in my mind, clear and bright. A golden temple, deep in the jungle. It sat at the edge of a huge river, overlooking the foliage.

The Amazon River.

Information flowed from the feather into my mind. Whoever had owned this feather had recently been at a temple in the Amazon jungle. El Dorado.

Holy fates, El Dorado?

But what did these murders have to do with El Dorado? And with me? If my new demon powers were tied up with El Dorado somehow, I needed to go there.

"You're going to have to give that up." The deep voice made a shiver race up my spine.

I looked up. Maximus the gladiator stood right next to me, his back pressed against the alley wall.

For such a huge man, he'd approached with complete silence. He positively towered over me, his dark gaze moving between the feather and my face. His scent wrapped around me, soap and cedar and man. I resisted sucking in a deep breath, but it was delightful.

He held out a big hand that looked like it could break trees in half. "Hand it over."

"No."

At my side, the raccoon watched closely.

I really shouldn't be arguing with the man who'd seen my dark magic, but I couldn't give up this feather, either. It was my only clue, and what gave him the right to take it from me?

"Why were you in The Vaults last night?" I demanded. "It seemed like you were waiting for the demons."

"Not waiting. Tracking."

"Tracking the demons and their monster?"

He nodded. "I was hired by the Order of the Magica to hunt these demons after one of their own was killed. A mage named Kevin Moreny. I liked him. Good kid."

I paled. Order of the Magica?

Oh crap. The very people I was afraid of. *Perfect.*

My mind raced as my skin chilled. I had to pretend I wasn't afraid of the Order. I focused on the dead person, which was terrible enough. "He really died?"

He nodded, the gesture sharp and his eyes dark. His harshly beautiful features were very slightly softened in grief. But only for a moment. A second later, they hardened. I felt like I'd seen beneath the mask, and I didn't hate the man under there.

This man, though? This man, I was wary of. He knew about the darkness in my soul.

"I'm sorry about Kevin." My mind raced. That meant these demons were serial killers...or at the very least working for one. And I was supposed to be like them, according to the demon I'd killed? That was almost worse than the soul-devouring part of this situation. "Do you know why they targeted him? Was his death like...this?"

I didn't know how to delicately ask *were his intestines also spilled all over the road?*

"Exactly like this. And no, I don't know why. A week ago, he was attacked and left like them." He nodded toward the bodies, his eyes sharp. "The Order knows nothing, so they hired me for the job. And personally, I want answers."

The cold determination in his voice sent a shudder down my spine. "Yet you came to help Jude with training today?"

"I'm freelance. She hired me for this job before the Order got in touch about the murders. The deaths take precedence, but coming here had the added bonus of giving me access to the Protectorate records."

"Ah, so you traded with Jude. In exchange for access to our records on giant monsters, you would train the new recruits."

"You. I was brought in to train *you*, since you're supposed to have no magic. Jude thought some extra fighting skills would come in handy." His gaze turned thoughtful. "But that's not the case, is it? You do have magic."

"I have no idea what you're talking about. So, you don't know who is sending the birds?"

"Don't try to change the subject."

"We have bigger issues than my magic. Like these murderers. You've really found no clues?"

"None." His gaze dropped to the feather. "That's the first solid lead I've had in a week. I need you to hand it over. And we're not done discussing the issue of your strange magic."

I clutched it tighter. "It was the demon. His own magic backfired on him. And I'm not giving you this feather. I need answers, too."

There was more I could learn from the feather, more clues I could reveal with the psychometros potion. I might need it to find my way to El Dorado.

"Why would you need answers?"

What could I tell him? That some mysterious note had made this my business? Or that the dark magic would devour my soul if I didn't get answers from the murderous demons themselves?

Neither of those were good options, but one version of the truth probably wasn't so bad.

"With my psychometros potion, I can track this feather and find out exactly where it's been. So I don't want to give it up."

His gaze sharpened. "Really? Is that what the licking was about?"

I scowled, wishing I'd developed a less ridiculous way to interact with the psychometros potion. But I hadn't because that had been the easiest way, so I was going to have to try to play this one off.

"Exactly. I developed it." It was one of my proudest accomplishments, actually.

"A true psychometros potion? I thought those didn't exist."

"There's one now. And only I can use it. So I suggest you leave me alone and go get one of those other feathers." I hiked my thumb back toward the crime scene where members of the PITs were finding other feathers. "You don't need this one."

"But perhaps I need you."

My cheeks heated, and I hated myself for it. I really didn't want to think of him that way.

"And *you* need *me* to keep your strange dark magic a secret."

Oh, that went downhill fast. I barely resisted wincing. He saw straight to the heart of the matter, didn't he? "I don't, actually. I told you, that was just the demon. His magic went haywire. I've never seen anything like it."

He was too smart to believe that. I could see it in his eyes.

Which meant I needed to get the hell away from him. What exactly did he think was going on with me? And would he turn me in to the Order of the Magica? After my time in captivity with the Rebel Gods, no way I was going to any prison. I'd die first.

I looked around for an escape, and caught sight of Jude walking toward me, her eyes keen on the feather in my hand.

She stopped in front of us. "What are you doing with that?"

"I've created a psychometros potion." I held up the feather. "I can track where this has been. I saw a temple in the jungle. El Dorado."

Her eyes widened. "You really created a potion that can read information from objects?"

"I did." I was the only one who'd managed that. Sheer luck, or fate. Some skill, definitely. All three, probably. And it was going to help me find the answers I so desperately needed.

Hedy, the R&D witch with lavender hair and an ever-changing array of flowy dresses, appeared out of nowhere. "Did I hear psychometros potion? Does it really work?"

I nodded, and her eyes brightened.

Jude and Hedy demanded a breakdown of the potion's abilities, how it reacted only with my saliva, and a full synopsis of what the feather had told me so far. Maybe I could convince them to let me get the heck out of Dodge for a while. Get away from Maximus and his damned training.

"So I was thinking that I could go hunt for the monster." I put on my most competent and serious expression. "I could find out where it's been by using my potion, and report back with information that might help us stop it." Even better, I could get away from Maximus.

Hedy looked torn, while Jude looked thoughtful.

I held up the feather. "Remember, I'm the only one who can track this using the potion. I'll go alone, and I don't need help. I'll travel light and fast and report back with anything I learn. There's nothing to lose, and I'm sure everyone else is really busy."

"They are," Jude said. "There have been reports of other attacks. They're tracking them down. We don't know if they are by these monsters or others, but hopefully we'll catch one in the act."

I nodded, feeling Maximus watching me keenly. "I can do it, Jude. I know it's rare to send out a trainee, but I promise to be careful. And you know I'm skilled. I can handle this."

It took a while, but eventually, Jude nodded. "You're like your sisters, Rowan. Perhaps you're slow to come into your powers"—I stifled a wince at the words—"but you're getting there. You have natural skill that most trainees don't. Consider this a test for the Academy."

"Thank you." Elation made me feel light as a balloon.

"But you'll go with Maximus." She looked at him for confirmation, and of course the bastard nodded.

My grin dropped. "I don't need help."

She turned to me. "You need backup. This will be dangerous. And he's hunting answers on behalf of the Order. If you team up, he can even help train you. Kill two birds with one stone. And it frees up the rest of the PITs to try to intercept new attacks."

Shit, shit, shit.

Everything she'd said made sense. There was no way for me to fight it. How could I make it work to my advantage?

I'd be able to keep an eye on him while getting answers, so maybe it wasn't all bad. I'd just keep the dark magic under control and prove to him that I was normal. I'd fix myself and solve a murder, and he'd realize that I'm not a threat.

This could actually be good. "Thanks, Jude. I promise to find answers."

"I know you will. You said you're headed to El Dorado?"

"The monsters were there according to the vision that the potion gave me. I've heard rumors that El Dorado is supposed to be somewhere on the Amazon River, and the vision confirmed that. There aren't many supernatural settlements down there. I can head down and ask around, maybe get a few more visions that can help pinpoint the location."

She nodded. "I've heard it's upriver from The Caipora's Den, a little village deep in the jungle. I don't have any contacts, but you can probably find a boat captain to take you."

"I have plenty of transport charms," Maximus said. "We can be there in minutes."

I shot him an impressed glance. Transport charms were notoriously hard to come by, but he had *plenty*?

"Just be careful," Jude said. "It's dangerous out there."

Dangerous? Oh yeah, I was aware. *Well* aware.

Jude and Hedy left, and I looked at Maximus. "I'll meet you at the front of the castle in twenty minutes, all right? I need to grab some things."

I had to stop by my place to get a bag of potion bombs. This was too dangerous, and my belt full of tiny potion vials wouldn't cut it.

He nodded and strode away, and I sagged.

Good luck with that.

I jumped, having forgotten the racoon. He'd been sitting on the dumpster all this time, watching us.

I turned to him. "Thanks."

Without another word, I left. Just before I departed the alley, I turned back, catching sight of the raccoon.

He gave me a look and made a V-shape with two tiny fingers that he pointed between us, going back and forth. *I'm watching you. Your trash is ours.*

Ours? I searched for other raccoons, and wondered if I'd invited a whole group of them to raid my trash bin.

Oh boy. My life was going off the rails.

5

THIRTY MINUTES LATER, AFTER COLLECTING MY BAG FULL OF potion bombs, I stepped through the portal created by Maximus's transport charm. We arrived just as dusk fell, stepping into the thick heat. It filled my lungs with warmth, reminding me of long-ago days in Death Valley.

The jungle rustled around us, massive leaves shifting on the breeze as animals screeched in the distance. We stood at the edge of a fairly large town called The Caipora's Den.

The brown, wooden buildings of the town blended into the jungle. Vines climbed over many of them, threatening to take them back to nature. Golden lights glowed in a few of the windows, but the street was quiet.

"Where is everyone?" I peered around, not seeing a single soul.

A massive cheer rose up from somewhere down the street, the sound of dozens of voices raised together. They sounded bloodthirsty.

"Well, that answers that," I murmured, and started off down the street.

Maximus easily kept pace with me, his long strides eating up the ground. It was hard to ignore his presence, but I did my best.

Of course I failed. I kept darting glances at him, as mistrustful of him as he was of me. Tension prickled between us, keeping me on my toes.

The middle of the street was muddy. The road was made of packed dirt and probably flooded every time it rained. We stuck to the wooden walkways that lined the fronts of the old buildings. A faint haze of magic floated on the air, the mingled scents of different supernaturals all clustered together. Some of the buildings had clear signs of magic—potions shops and the like—but otherwise, it looked like a fairly normal place.

The noise of a crowd grew louder as we neared the end of town. Up close, I could see golden lights gleaming on the jungle behind some buildings.

I nodded toward a narrow street between two buildings. "Let's cut through this alley."

"You're quite bossy."

I grinned. "I know what I'm doing."

Maximus gave me a quizzical look, then slipped in front of me, seeming determined to lead the way, like he wanted to get the jump on any danger. It was fine with me. If he somehow got ambushed by some demons and killed, then no one besides my sisters would know about my deadly power.

A win-win, as far as I was concerned.

But even as I thought it, guilt bloomed inside me.

He was a decent dude. Though he was definitely dangerous to my well-being, I didn't like the thought of something bad happening to a good person.

The fizzle of attraction had nothing to do with it, of course.

Waaaaay too soon for that.

The alley was so narrow and dark that I couldn't see around his wide shoulders, but the sound of the cheering crowd grew loud enough that it felt like we were in a stadium. There was definitely some kind of sporting event going on.

As soon as I exited the alley, I caught sight of a raised fight ring in the middle of the clearing. Two massive men went at it with just their fists, while dozens of supernaturals stood around the ring, cheering and shouting. Lights hung from wires overhead, illuminating the whole spectacle.

"I guess there's not much else to do in the jungle," I said.

"And gamble." Maximus nodded toward a building to the left. A sign overhead said something in Portuguese that I had to imagine said *Casino.*

"You speak Portuguese?"

"And a few other languages." He didn't stick around to provide any more detail, just cut straight through the crowd to an open-air bar near the building.

I followed, searching the space for anyone who might be able to give us a ride up the river. No one was wearing a captain's hat, however, and I wasn't particularly surprised.

I joined Maximus at the bar, squeezing in beside him and a smelly guy with green skin and yellow eyes. Some kind of snake hybrid shifter, if I had to guess. I edged closer to Maximus.

He leaned on the bar and smiled at the bartender, turning up the charm. It didn't make him look friendly—I wasn't sure anything would—but it made him look sexy as hell.

The pretty blonde bartender seemed to agree with me. She bent over the bar and smiled at him, leaning on her arms in a way that pushed up her boobs. Next to me, the green snake man drooled.

Men.

I had to admit she looked pretty good. I just hoped she was friendly enough to give us the info we wanted.

"Two of whatever you've got on tap, please." Maximus's voice had taken on an even huskier timbre than normal.

I shot him a sidelong glance.

He was *totally* seducing the bartender.

"Coming right up." She smiled and turned, sashaying away toward the taps.

I nudged him in the ribs, leaning close enough to smell the heady scent of his skin. "Laying it on a little thick, aren't you?"

His dark eyes met mine. "Jealous?"

Annoyance flashed through me. Maybe I was, and I didn't like it. I'd die before I'd let him know it, though. I gave him the most desperate look I could manage and leaned close, giving my voice an extra high pitch. "So jealous, baby. I wish you'd just throw me right up on this bar and take your big—"

He growled low in his throat, his eyes heating, and pressed a hand to my mouth. "Enough. You'll blow it for us."

I smirked, pretending not to enjoy the warm press of his hand against my lips, and pinched his waist. He was a wall of muscle, and it was hard to get much to pinch, but he got the picture and removed his hand.

As soon as his touch disappeared, I remembered our situation. He knew what I was. He could turn me in. I could never trust him.

All very simple, really.

I gestured to the bartender who was still filling the glasses. "See what you can get out of her with that pretty face."

He gave me an annoyed look and leaned over the bar, accepting the glasses with a smile. He passed an unidentifiable bill over the counter—Brazilian money, I had to guess— and from the bartender's expression, I had to assume it was a lot.

"Any chance you can point us to the most desperate riverboat captain in this place?" he asked. "Someone who will take us somewhere dangerous."

She pursed her lips, clearly thinking. "That'd have to be

Eloa. She'll be playing poker in the main building. Short girl, purple eyes, you can't miss her."

"Thanks, darling." Maximus's deep voice shivered over my nerve endings, and he wasn't even talking to me.

Blonde girl looked like she might actually jump on him.

All he'd done was ask her a question and say thanks.

What was it about this guy? It was like he was shooting out sex pheromones and every woman within hearing distance—me included, to my horror—was *way* interested.

I gave a disgusted sigh and grabbed my beer, then stalked away from the bar. Apparently I didn't look as threatening as I hoped, because no one cleared a path for me as I walked. I threw a few elbows and cleared the way, then stepped into the gambling hall.

Maximus appeared behind me, not saying a word. But I could tell it was him. I'd sense him if he were a mile away. And that annoyed me even more. Whatever connection we had between us was damned inconvenient. I didn't even *know* the guy. I shouldn't feel like this.

I took a big gulp of my icy beer as I surveyed the dimly lit interior of the building. Bare light bulbs hung from the ceiling, illuminating rickety tables and chairs. Almost every single one was full, gamblers hunched over their cards and staring intently at those around them.

"She's there." Maximus pointed toward a woman in the corner.

Her purple eyes glowed from all the way across the room, making her look like she was lit from within. Holy cow, the bartender had been right. You really couldn't miss Eloa. She had dark hair and skin and was ethereally beautiful. But her eyes... They blasted like they were lit with LEDs.

I slipped through the crowd, eyeing an empty chair at the table across from her. It was a four-top, and from the spread on the table, she was playing blackjack against the house. I'd played a few times as a kid, before I'd been abducted, and was damned good at it.

We stopped in front of the table, and Eloa looked up. The dealer was a hulking brute with magic that smelled like tree sap.

"Eloa?" Maximus asked.

"Who's asking?" she purred.

I'd almost guess she was some kind of cat shifter, but didn't think that was quite on the money.

"I'm Maximus, and this is Rowan Blackwood. We're looking for a ride up the river."

Her gaze shuttered. "I'm busy."

"We pay well," he said.

Her purple eyes sharpened on him. "How well?"

"Ten grand for a ride up to El Dorado."

Her two companions choked. She just laughed.

"Twenty?" he asked.

"It's not the money, big guy. No way in hell am I risking my life to get up to El Dorado. It's a death wish." She turned back to her cards, clearly done with us.

I glanced at Maximus, who frowned grimly. Eloa was deadly serious. No way was she going to take us up to El Dorado.

I slipped into the chair across from her. "Can I play?"

Maximus's strong hand gripped my shoulder. He didn't seem to like this, but I didn't care.

I had a plan.

Eloa gave me a critical look. "Why?"

"Because I want to win some money?"

"You need to have money to play."

I raised a hand so that it hovered over my shoulder, a signal to Maximus. A painful second passed as he decided if he was going to give me the money I was so obviously demanding. I was about to kick him in the shin when a wad of bills landed in my palm.

A tiny flare of warmth lit in my chest. He trusted me. Or he was bad with money.

Either way, I was in.

I looked down at the bills he'd handed me. Eloa's sharp eyes narrowed on the wad of cash I sorted through. Greed glittered within.

It was a ton of freaking money, and I peeled off two hundred-dollar bills and passed them to the dealer. He handed me some chips, his eyes bored, then dealt out the cards.

I looked at my card that lay face-down, then smiled. Not a bad pair. That would make this quicker. The first rule of card sharking, as I'd developed them when I was a kid, was to be totally average. Not good, not bad. I was a good actress and even better at counting cards. Math had always been my thing, and for a while, I'd supported my sisters with my abilities. At least until the local bar had figured out what I was doing. I'd only been thirteen, so they hadn't given me the usual beating. But I hadn't been able to play anymore.

I looked at Eloa. "So, you're good at this?"

She grinned, shark-like, and pride radiated from her. "The best."

Right then. I'd have to be good. But she was proud, and that could work in my favor.

The first round went quickly. I almost won, and that was the point. We both lost the next to the house, and I spared a glance up at Maximus. He looked annoyed, which was to be expected.

Eloa's sharp gaze kept darting between the two of us. "Why do you want to go to El Dorado?"

"For the gold, of course," I said.

"It's cursed." She shuffled the next hand. "Take one piece of it, and you become the walking dead."

"I'm not worried about that." I accepted my cards and peeked at the one that was facedown. Only a moron would lose with these. Looked like I was going to win this round.

"Then you're a moron."

"Occasionally, but not in this." I rejected another card. "Also, I'm desperate."

The round finished, and I won. It was the victory of a lucky idiot, however, and she knew it. So far, I'd mostly sucked. Not so badly that she'd expect card sharking, but bad enough that I'd probably lured her into my trap. I scraped my winnings toward me.

We played another round, which she won. I made sure to keep Maximus's entire lump of cash sitting right in front of me on the table. Eloa's eyes kept darting to it.

Yep, she was desperate. Maybe she had some debts.

Once again, Maximus's strong hand landed on my shoulder. He was getting annoyed, but I wasn't done yet. We were on our third round since the dealer had shuffled, and I had a good idea of what was coming. He dealt our cards, and I peeked at mine, pleased.

I looked at Eloa. "Want to make a side bet on this hand?"

"Why?"

"You could win some more money." I set a pile of cash on the table between us, then looked at the dealer. Though we were betting on the outcome of this game, the money wasn't technically *part* of the game. He looked away, apparently used to such things.

Eloa's eyes narrowed. "So if I win this hand, I get that money. And if you win, I suppose you want a ride upriver to El Dorado?"

Eloa wasn't stupid, that was for sure. "Yep."

"What if the house wins?"

"Then we're both out of luck. I keep my money and you don't go up the river."

She debated, chewing her lip. Eloa peeked at her cards, then nodded.

I tapped the table. "Hit me."

Tension crackled across my skin as I waited for the dealer to hand me the card. I'd counted right and the odds were in my favor, but you just never knew.

The next card landed in front of me, and I stifled a smile.

Jackpot.

Eloa took her card, then grimaced and pushed her cards across the table. "You win."

I stood. "Let's get a move on, then."

Eloa rose, eyeing me suspiciously.

I ignored the look. "Lead the way."

She nodded sharply, and pushed her way through the crowd. I collected the cash from the table and handed it back to Maximus, then followed Eloa out of the crowded bar.

The jungle embraced us in its damp heat as we stepped out onto the boardwalk. Eloa had exited through the side of the building, and it was quiet, the roar of the crowd dampened to a dull roar.

"My boat's docked at the river."

"Do we need to wait until morning to depart?" Maximus asked.

"Nope. No good time to travel that part of the river, so might as well get this over with."

"I like how you think." I grinned, squinting into the distance and hoping to see some monkeys. I'd never been to the jungle that I could recall. There were a lot of times during my captivity with the Rebel Gods that I couldn't remember, but I didn't count anything from that time as a real experience. "How long have you been running your boat on the river? And what is it you do?"

"Smuggling, mostly." She grinned at me. "Been doing it about six months."

"Just six?" Shit.

"Yep. You sure you want to throw your lot in with me? Not sure I'm the most qualified."

"I like a challenge."

Eloa scowled. I had a feeling she was lying about the whole six months bit, anyway. At least I hoped. I shot Maximus a glance. He shrugged, clearly thinking the same thing. What other choice did we have?

"What are you?" I asked.

"Bruxa." She glanced at me and must've caught sight of my confused expression. "Witch."

"Ah."

"You?"

"Um." Well, shit. Of course she'd return the question. I had been a telekinetic. Now... "Potion master."

Kinda. She accepted the answer, though, so I took it.

She led us down to the river, where two dozen boats of various sizes and styles were tied off to the old wooden docks. The water moved sluggishly along, the river so wide that it could have been a lake. Night animals were even louder over here, with a cacophony of monkeys and bugs and birds that all blended together to create a riotous symphony.

"That'll be the *Kilbourne* right there." Eloa pointed toward a boat that was tied off to one of the middle docks.

It was one of the bigger vessels, at least forty feet long, with a low, flat deck and a steamship stack right in the middle. A huge paddlewheel hung off the back.

"Holy crap, it's a steamboat?" I asked. "Aren't those extinct?"

Eloa shrugged. "I like it. And it runs partially on magic now, anyway. Not like I'm chopping a ton of wood or hauling coal or anything."

I followed her onto the boat. There were no structures on the deck other than a pilothouse and the thing that burned the wood for the steam engines. A boiler, I thought it was called.

There was a flat wooden roof built overhead, but there were no walls. A hammock hung right in the middle, no doubt where Eloa slept.

Near the bow, a monkey sat, eating what looked to be a ham sandwich. I grinned. I'd wanted to see one of these suckers, but I hadn't expected him to be eating a ham sandwich.

"Hey, Ted," Eloa said. "We're headed upriver to El Dorado."

The monkey just glared at her.

Eloa turned to us. "We'll get started now. Stay alert. Things should be fine for the first little bit, but it could get sticky after that."

The monkey gave a wheezy laugh.

"Ted has a weird sense of humor." Eloa went to the middle of the boat and reached into a barrel that was strapped down to the deck. She pulled out a blue rock, then chucked it in the boiler. The thing blazed to life, and the engines started pumping. The paddlewheel creaked and groaned, finally spinning and kicking up water.

Eloa threw off the lines and steered the boat away from the dock.

I joined Maximus at the bow, leaning over the rail to look out at the dark river. Moonlight gleamed on the water, and the jungle rustled on either side.

My skin prickled with awareness, and I spoke to distract myself. "This is not what I anticipated."

"I'm not sure anyone could anticipate a steamboat on the Amazon. Not these days, at least."

I glanced back. Eloa stared out of the pilothouse, her eyes keen on the river. Ted the Monkey sat in the hammock, glaring at us. Mean monkey.

We rode in silence for a while. Though I stood only two feet from him, it felt closer. He had such a presence that it was impossible to ignore. His power radiated from him, feeling like a caress against my skin. I scowled into the distance.

"Speaking of not anticipating," he said. "You are definitely not what I expected."

Honestly, *I* wasn't what *I* expected. This new magic shocked the hell out of me, too. Not that I could tell him that.

"Not just the dark magic, which we can discuss later." His gaze turned serious at that. He wasn't going to forget, and he didn't trust me. The truth was clear enough. "But you did well in the fight at the Protectorate."

"Of course I did." *That* was one thing I was confident of.

"Why are you such a good fighter?"

"Training." I didn't want to mention that my missing magic was why I'd dedicated myself to becoming such a good fighter. Anyway, I'd always had a knack for it. No harm in telling him that bit of my history, to give him something to throw him off the scent. "I spent my teenage years in Death Valley. My sisters and I made trips across the desert, driving people out to Hider's Haven."

I could feel his gaze move from the river to me. "That's one of the most dangerous stretches of land in the world. You did that as a kid?"

I shrugged. "Didn't have much choice. Had to make a living, didn't we?"

"Not traditionally, no. Most kids have parents to take care of them at that age."

"Well, we didn't. Our dad had been gone since we were babies, and my mom died when we were thirteen. We were on our own at that point." And running from the Rebel Gods, who'd killed my mom in their hunt for us. We'd had to keep a low profile, and Death Valley had been the way to do that. It was so miserable, almost no one went there. "Anyway, it was a good time, and it taught me some stuff." I shot him a sidelong glance. He looked damned good in the moonlight, all strong and manly and highlighted by the moon. His suspicion of me radiated from him, though, kind of killing the mood. "I suppose you had nice parents? PTA, home-baked cookies, dad home at six for dinner?"

"No. I grew up in a different time."

"What do you mean? Like, the eighties?"

He chuckled and the low sound reached inside me and tugged. I cleared my throat, suddenly awkward.

"No. I was born in AD 89."

"Wait, what?"

"I grew up on a farm in southern Germany. Life was different then."

"Holy shit, how are you alive now?" None of this made any sense.

"It's a bit of a long story. Not very interesting."

"Somehow, I doubt that." Though I definitely believed he didn't share it often. "You'd have to be a god to live that long." In fact, his power *had* been strong. I eyed him up and down. *Was* he a god? "I want to know the story."

So do we.

The voice sounded from near my feet. I glanced down to see the raccoon from the Grassmarket sitting there, along with a possum and a badger friend.

My jaw dropped. "How did you get here? And who are they?"

You promised us your trash, remember?

I remembered that 'ours' he'd said as I'd walked away from the alley, but hadn't expected a badger and a possum. "Yeah, but—"

"Are you talking to that raccoon?"

I looked up at Maximus. "I am, but it's not as weird as it

looks." Okay, maybe it was that weird, but I didn't know what else to say.

I'm not weird, I'm—

The boat shifted underfoot, cutting off everyone's words.

"Hang on!" Eloa called.

"What's happening?" I gripped the railing tight as the boat heaved on the river, the bow dipping low then coming up again.

"No idea!" Eloa shouted. "Get ready, though. Probably not gonna be fun!"

In front of us, the water rippled, then exploded outward as a giant snake reared up. The creature was bigger than the boat, its fangs as long as my arms. It loomed above us, death incarnate, then reared back to strike.

6

"*Merda*!" Eloa cried. "It's the *Boitatá*! Don't look into its eyes for more than a few seconds! It could blind you!"

I caught only the barest glimpse of flame-red eyes and quickly looked downward. My heart thundered as I jammed my hand into the pouch of potion bombs slung around my hip. I grabbed the first one and kept the snake in my peripheral vision. Panic prickled my skin as I hurled the bomb at the snake's head. As it flew, I saw that the glass was blue.

Good, my strongest one.

I called it the Murder Bomb because it was full of a rare venom from a tiny lizard, and it would take out even the strongest demons. It should at least stun this guy.

The glass exploded against the upper part of the snake's body—he was as wide around as a truck—but he didn't even flinch.

"Nothing can penetrate its skin!" Eloa shouted.

Crap.

Maximus sprinted toward the side of the boat, his sword gripped in his hand. He must have drawn it from the ether or something, because he hadn't been carrying it earlier. Or maybe he'd conjured it. Either way, he seemed determined to leap onto the snake, but as soon as he heard Eloa's words, he halted.

He searched the surrounding jungle, and I did the same, looking frantically for a plan.

The snake reared its head back to strike.

Despite Eloa's warning, I couldn't help but sneak a peek at it. Slowly, my vision began to dim, and I forced my head down.

I caught sight of Maximus. A large shield appeared on his left arm. Conjured, I had to bet. My sisters and I had bought expensive spells to allow us to store our weapons in the ether and draw them when necessary, but it looked like Maximus had another skill entirely.

The snake pulled its head back a bit farther, then struck. Eloa screamed and jerked the wheel, but the boat was too slow to maneuver out of the snake's way.

As the beast's head neared the boat, moving so fast it was hard to see, Maximus sprinted toward it and leapt into the air. He slammed his shield against the side of the snake's head, and the creature spun away, stunned. It crashed down through the bushes and slammed to the ground.

Maximus landed back on deck with a thud, then whirled to face us. The snake lay still, its massive head resting on a bush near the river.

"It won't stay down for long," Maximus said.

We needed another plan.

My gaze caught on the massive vines hanging from the trees that towered alongside the river. The snake shifted, blinking groggily.

We were out of time. "Let's tie him up with the vines. Hold him back."

Maximus turned to inspect the vines. The snake was slowly rising, shaking its head back and forth as if trying to get its senses together.

We can help! The raccoon's voice sounded from behind me.

I'd almost forgotten he was there.

"Sure." It was obvious from my tone that I didn't know what three small dumpster divers could do.

We were in the circus. This is our jam!

The circus? I'd take any help we could get, so I nodded. "Eloa, direct the boat toward shore and run alongside."

"This better work!" Skepticism sounded in her voice.

Frankly, I couldn't blame her. I was feeling a bit iffy myself.

The boat neared the shore, and I sprinted toward a large box near the railing, then jumped up and leapt off the box so I could grab onto one of the vines that hung low over the water. I sailed through the air and grabbed onto another vine, swinging like Tarzan. Maximus did the same, jumping much farther than I had.

I scrambled up the vine, my hands occasionally slipping on the surface. Every time they did, my stomach fell.

A quick glance at the snake showed that he'd almost entirely regained his senses. He was doing the rear-back-and-strike thing that seemed to be a snake's signature move.

A branch hovered above the snake's head, and three tiny figures caught my eye.

The raccoon, possum, and badger landed on the snake's head. The creature hissed and thrashed, trying to throw them off. But they clung tight.

Quick! While he's distracted! the raccoon shouted.

Holy fates, my life was weird.

I met Maximus's gaze and he nodded. "I'll get to the other side!"

He swung from vine to vine, determined to reach the other side of the snake so we could come at it from two different angles, hopefully trapping it against the shore with the vines.

I scrambled up onto a tree limb and gripped my vine tight. We'd have to time it just right.

The snake was still thrashing, but fortunately it wasn't striking our boat. Maximus climbed onto a limb on the other side of the snake, about forty feet up the riverbank.

"Now!" I shouted, and leapt off the tree limb, clutching the vine tight. I hurtled through the air, the wind whipping at my hair. My vine carried me around the snake's lower body, and Maximus passed by above me.

It's working!

I didn't spare the raccoon a glance as my vine caught on the snake and dragged him against the shore. I hurtled toward some bushes, suddenly realizing that I hadn't planned my dismount.

Life comes at you fast sometimes, and I slammed into the bushes, losing my grip on my vine. I plowed through the leaves and landed in the spongy ground. A massive beetle stared at me.

"You're the size of a house cat," I muttered as my brains rattled around inside my head. I scrambled to my feet and grabbed my vine, then pulled it around a tree to tie it off. Hopefully it would trap the snake for at least a few minutes.

Finished, I sprinted back toward the shore. To my left, something thrashed through the foliage. The snake.

Hurry! He's stunned, but not for long!

I looked up to see the Menacing Menagerie leaping across the tree branches as we raced back to the shore. The raccoon led the way, but the possum and badger were close behind. The light of battle gleamed in the badger's eyes, while the possum just looked joyful.

I reached the shore. The bottom half of the snake's body thrashed in the water, while the top half was temporarily pinned to the ground. The steamboat was already twenty feet down shore and didn't look like it was turning around. Maximus was already halfway up a tree ahead of me.

"Get a vine and swing back!" he shouted.

I scaled a tree, moving faster than I ever had in my life, and grabbed a vine.

I leapt, swinging through the air and praying that I landed on the deck of the *Kilbourne*.

Of course I didn't.

I got close, though, releasing the vine and landing in the river with a splash. Warm, dark water closed around me, and I kicked to the surface.

The first thing I heard when my head broke through made my blood chill.

"Piranha!"

My heart leapt into my throat, and I kicked forward, racing for the boat. I cut through the water so fast that I arrived seconds later, grabbing for the side as the current dragged at me. Maximus leaned over and lowered his hand. I stretched my arm up to him, and he grasped my hand, hauling me over the side railing.

I flopped onto the deck, panting.

The sound of Eloa's laughter filtered toward me.

I looked up, blinking water out of my eyes. "There were no piranhas, were there?"

She wiped tears from her bright eyes as she looked at me. "Probably not, but you never know."

I shot her the hairy eyeball, and she just laughed harder. "Well, you did fine with the snake." Her eyes widened on something behind us. "Time to go."

She darted toward the barrel of magical blue fuel rocks and grabbed three, then chucked them into the boiler. A plume of smoke burst from the boiler, and the boat shot forward.

I turned, looking toward the snake.

The creature was heaving itself back toward the river.

"Faster!" I shouted to Eloa.

"This is as fast as it goes!"

We cut through the water, racing away from the snake. The Menacing Menagerie came to sit beside me where I was still collapsed on the deck, panting.

The raccoon sat on his butt and held out his little hand. *I'm Romeo.*

I shook his tiny paw. "Good to meet you, Romeo. I'm Rowan."

Romeo pointed at the possum. *That's Poppy. And the badger is Eloise.*

They were the oddest trio I'd ever seen. The possum was small and gray, with a severely pointed nose and a red flower behind her ear. She gave me a suspicious look, while the badger growled, sharp teeth threatening.

"How come you can talk?"

I'm the leader of the Magical Menagerie.

"The what?"

We're the Magical Menagerie, the most famous all-animal circus in Europe. He grinned, and I expected that it was supposed to be charming. It kind of was.

The possum hissed.

That was not charming.

The raccoon sighed. *Fine, Poppy. We're no longer the Magical Menagerie. We're the Menacing Menagerie.*

"Who do you menace?"

Rubbish bins, mostly.

"Really? Why'd you leave the circus to menace rubbish bins?"

As Poppy is trying to point out, the money corrupted us. We decided to quit to focus on the finer things in life. His little paw reached over to rub the top of the trash bin that sat lashed to the railing. The gesture was distinctly loving.

"Is trash a finer thing in life?"

He grinned toothily at me. *The finest. Poppy thinks she loves trash most, but really, it's me. Eloise is a peacekeeper, except when she's really fighting.*

"Well, thanks for the help. Seems like you're good at menacing more than trash. That snake wouldn't want to meet you again, I bet."

He grinned, showing his little fangs.

I nodded at Poppy and Eloise in greeting, then dragged myself to my feet. Water dripped down my legs. Every inch of me was soaked, and it sucked.

"Hey, come here," Eloa shouted.

I turned and scowled. "What now?"

"Fine, be grumpy." Eloa held out her hand toward me, palm up. Her magic flared on the air, bringing with it the scent of bananas and rich earth. It was a weird combo.

When warm air blasted from her palm and dried my clothes in seconds, I decided I didn't care how weird it was. "Thank you."

I ran my hands through my hair, delighted to feel it totally dry.

"You've got some interesting sidekicks," Maximus said.

I glanced back at the Menacing Menagerie, who were now sitting with Eloa's monkey and sharing some ham sandwiches. Poppy looked a bit morose, as if she wished she'd pulled it out of some dumpster somewhere.

"Yeah, don't know how they chose me, but I'll take them." Actually, that wasn't quite true. I did know. Both of my sisters had animal sidekicks as well. They'd gotten them when they'd begun the transition to Dragon God. Maybe I was transitioning?

I focused inward, trying to identify any new magic that might be lurking in my soul.

There was just the darkness, though.

I really hoped it was a fluke—some horrible curse from my time with the Rebel Gods. I didn't want this darkness to be my gods-given powers. Because what would that make me?

Something evil, definitely.

I didn't need, or want, any part of that crap.

"Help yourself to sandwiches," Eloa said. "Ted can show you where the stuff is."

My stomach grumbled at the word, and I grinned at her. "Thanks, Eloa. You rock."

"You're easily bought," Eloa said.

"If there's food, then yes." I shot her one more big smile, then joined Ted.

The little monkey pointed out the cooler containing ham and the loaf of bread sitting on top. It was simple, but delicious. Maximus and I ate in silence, but I couldn't help wondering about his past. I wanted to ask, but I was too busy stuffing my face. Fighting giant snakes worked up an appetite, apparently.

Due to the extra input of fuel, the boat made quick time down the river. The thing went so fast that I worried the paddlewheel would spin off. Finally, though, we slowed.

"Going to give the *Kilbourne* a break," Eloa said. "Go at a more normal speed."

As much as I wanted to make quick time, I didn't want to lose the paddlewheel. And Eloa didn't look like the kind of woman who took suggestions well.

She joined us for a sandwich as the boat drifted along. "Don't worry, there's autopilot at this speed."

"On a boat this old?" Maximus asked.

"Magic." She bit into her sandwich.

I wanted to ask more about the spell, but a ghostly wail cut off my words.

Eloa's purple eyes widened, and she lowered her sandwich. "*Merda*."

I jumped to my feet, my skin chilling at the sound.

Eloa paled, her dark skin turning to ash. "The Caipora."

I spun in a circle, searching the dark jungle. Moonlight gleamed on the water and jungle, but I saw no threats. I could hear them, though, and it made my heart thunder.

"What are the Caipora?" Maximus conjured a sword.

"Spirits who haunt trespassers. *We're* trespassers." She hurried to a long, low trunk that was bolted to the deck and began to dig inside of it. She withdrew three simple iron swords, each coated with rust. The blades were so dull they couldn't cut cheese. She tossed one at me, and I grabbed it, catching it by the blade and not receiving a single cut. "Use that to kill them."

I inspected the blade, then looked up at her doubtfully. "You sure about that?"

"They're ghosts, and those blades are enchanted. The Caipora are like Phantoms, but they *can* be killed."

I shuddered. "Phantoms?"

I freaking hated Phantoms. The miserable beasts made you face your worst fears and nightmares, then fed off your energy.

"Phantoms." Eloa nodded. "The Caipora will show you the most horrible things from your past, then when you are weak, they pounce. It takes them less than a minute to suck out all of your lifeforce. But they also carry weapons that will wound."

We don't have swords, so see you later. Romeo gave me an apologetic look, then disappeared, along with Poppy and Eloise.

I couldn't say that I blamed them.

"Be alert." Eloa returned to the pilothouse, her sword gripped in her hand.

I joined Maximus at the bow, and we stood back to back, inspecting the jungle. My skin crawled as the wailing of the Caipora grew louder.

They appeared seconds later, pale, ghostly forms with jet-black eyes and gaping mouths. Cold filled me to my bones, sending ice through my veins.

I couldn't help the thoughts that rose in my mind. Memories of my capture, of my captivity.

In front of me, the Caipora drifted closer, floating over the river until they were nearly to us. Then they shifted, changing form. They pantomimed my past, and I saw myself, raising my hands and using terrible magic on behalf of the Rebel Gods. Threatening my sisters.

Horror rose in me, a black hole that threatened to devour my heart. Fear and misery flowed through me, bringing back all the memories of my captivity. I'd been forced to do terrible things. Horrible things.

The Caipora drifted in front of me, recreating my past and dredging up the worst of my memories. Things I'd forced away were surging to the surface.

My legs nearly buckled.

"Come at me!" I screamed, desperately wanting the Caipora to start the fight. This was torture. Their reenactment was a spike to the chest. I spun, trying to look away.

Instead, I caught sight of another scene.

The Caipora were acting out Maximus's worst memory. It was in a gladiator ring, and rows of men were kneeling. An executioner stood with his axe, ready to behead over two dozen people. Maximus was among them.

I shuddered and turned away. Somehow, his was worse. I could only handle the pain of my own terrible past. No way I could also bear the pain of his.

Agony speared my mind as I tried to force away the horrible memories. But I couldn't. They played in the jungle around me, acted out by ghosts. They played within my mind as well, bringing back the feelings of pain and despair and horror.

When I looked up to face my own miserable past, the

Caipora broke apart. They rushed me, arms raised. I lunged for them, weakened by my grief and horror. How was it that it had such a physical effect?

I sucked in a ragged breath and raised my blade, swinging for the nearest Caipora. The beast was reaching out with ghostly white arms.

My rusty steel severed the limbs, and the creature shrieked, mouth gaping wide and dark. It wheeled away, but another replaced it, surging toward me. I sliced at its middle, taking it out, but the third carried a sword as well.

The ghost sliced its blade toward me, and I parried, blocking his steel with my own. The swords smashed together, the ghost's blade becoming corporeal on contact with my own.

I drew my sword back and swung, slicing the neck of my opponent. But two rushed me next, one slashing out with a dagger that cut deep into my arm.

Pain flared and blood spurted. I jabbed my weapon toward the creature's stomach, sinking my blade deep. It shrieked, an unearthly wail that surely made my ears bleed. I stumbled backward, swiping out with my sword.

Out of the corners of my eyes, I could see Maximus and Eloa fighting off their own ghosts.

One of the Caipora swung a blade at Maximus, slicing him right through the middle. But he didn't even flinch. The blade didn't hurt him at all—not like it had hurt me.

What the hell was he, if he couldn't be injured?

I had no time to think of it. More Caipora were surging toward me, as if I were the weaker link.

Three of them charged, and I swiped out with my blade, taking out one after another. They kept coming though. More and more. They surrounded me, half a dozen closing in. I cut and stabbed, but no longer had the range of movement required.

The ghosts reached out with transparent arms, grabbing and tugging. Everywhere they touched burned. I screamed and thrashed, swinging my blade and kicking out. I hurt them, managing to drive off some. But others came, too, overwhelming me.

Panic rose in my chest, and my magic flared.

From deep inside, the darkness rose. I didn't ask it to. I didn't call on it. But it came anyway, surging to the surface. A protective instinct that I couldn't deny.

It choked me, feeling foul inside my very soul. My eyes began to glow, brightening the faces of the ghosts who attacked. It felt like I was drawing from within as the magic filled up my body, filled up my soul.

Then it burst from me, exploding outward.

The Caipora shrieked and lunged backward, hissing and whirling. Some of them disintegrated right on the spot, their ghostly forms turning to ash. The rest raced away, disappearing within seconds.

I stood, panting. The horror of the memories made me feel empty inside.

I'd never before remembered with such clarity. But I'd relived it here, and the memories made me shake.

I looked up and caught sight of Maximus and Eloa's shocked gazes.

Shit.

Adrenaline pumped through my veins, driving off the thoughts of my terrible past.

They'd seen my dark magic. Maximus, for the second time.

7

ELOA TURNED AWAY, MUTTERING, "I'M NOT GOING TO ASK."

I sucked in an unsteady breath. What happened in the jungle stayed in the jungle, apparently. At least with her. I could live with that. Maybe I could even move here, if everything hit the fan.

Yeah, that sounded terrible.

I avoided looking at Maximus and pulled a tiny vial of healing potion out of my leather belt. As I dotted it on the stinging wound on my shoulder, I could feel Maximus's gaze on me.

Once the wound was tended to, I looked up at him.

"She might not ask, but I will," he said. "What the hell is going on with you?"

"Nothing." I felt stupid even saying it, since I'd been so obvious this time. I tried turning away anyway, hoping he'd get the picture.

He didn't. Instead, he followed me to the bow and leaned on the railing.

I stared out at the water, my mind racing.

Okay, so maybe this had been a bad idea. Before, he'd seen me do something creepy and weird. It could have been a fluke.

Now, he'd seen me do it twice.

How was I supposed to damage control that?

"What's going on, Rowan?"

I stayed silent, debating my options. Jumping overboard was the only one that appealed, and even that had the downside of piranhas. Maybe.

His brows lowered, and he frowned. "What's going on?"

"I don't know, exactly." I searched his face, trying to see past the good looks to what was beneath. I couldn't trust him, could I? He worked for the Order.

But I wasn't evil. My version of events—which was *true,* damn it—made me out to be a victim. On one hand, I hated that. *Hated it.* On the other hand, it made me not to blame.

If I wasn't to blame, maybe I wouldn't be reported to the Order of the Magica and sent to the Prison for Magical Miscreants.

Maybe.

Did I suck it up and swallow my pride, explaining my shitty situation and the years I'd spent in captivity?

Victim.

Victim.

Victim.

I liked the person I'd become. Powerful, in control. I might have no magic, but I was in control of my own destiny now.

Logically, I knew that admitting to my horrible past didn't take away who I was now. I'd just really liked shoving it down deep and not acknowledging it.

I wanted to keep hiding, but so far, that hadn't been working. I'd thought I could keep it under control when I'd agreed to come work with him, but I'd been wrong.

"Rowan, you need to explain. It can't be that bad."

I laughed. "Of course it can." I met his blue gaze. "I saw your past. You know as well as I that it can be that bad."

"If I show you mine, will you show me yours?"

My eyes flared wide, then I got it. "Ah, you'd explain that scene? And in exchange, I tell you what's up with me?"

He nodded.

"It'd better be good, then."

"It's pretty good."

It was something to consider. Right now, saying nothing made me look definitely evil. I had to tell him something—try to explain. And if I was going to do that, I might as well get a story out of him in exchange. And, if he was a total jerk and wanted to throw me into the Prison for Magical Miscreants, I had a forgetfulness potion I could try on him. It'd be really hard to get him to drink it, but I could manage if I was desperate enough.

Finally, I nodded. "You go first."

He leaned against the bow rail, turning to face the water. He didn't want to look at me while he spoke, and I got that. Boy, did I ever.

"I was kidnapped from my family farm when I was twelve," he said.

Oh, shit. Yeah, he knew about crappy pasts.

"The Romans were coming through, doing as they always did. And I was big for my age. Strong." He shot me a wry glance. "A lot of time with the plow."

I nodded as if I knew what that meant, but I didn't. Spending my youth farming in the freaking Dark Ages wasn't really in my repertoire.

"They took me to Rome, where I was sold as a slave. I ended up in the ring as a gladiator." His gaze riveted to my mouth. "Why are you smiling?"

"Oops." I slapped a hand over my mouth. "Sorry. I've been calling you a gladiator in my head. You just...look like one."

"I spent ten years in the ring. I don't think I'll lose the bearing."

"Ten *years?* That had to be so many matches."

"Over a thousand. I was the best." His eyes turned dark. "Which comes with a price."

"You had to kill." I could see from the grief and guilt in his gaze exactly what he meant.

"Kill my fellow slaves." He nodded. "Not every time. Not even most. But more than once is enough. Eventually, I couldn't take it anymore."

"You revolted." My mind went back to the memory reenacted by the Caipora. "You led a revolt, and it failed. So you and your men were supposed to be executed in the middle of the arena. That was your Caipora memory."

He nodded. "You're quick. And correct. Over half of us died in the revolt. The rest were meant to be beheaded to make an example."

"How'd you escape?"

"I used all the skills I'd ever learned. I killed the executioner and many of the guards. I was about to kill the emperor when I was struck down by his guards. I was bleeding out in the dirt when Virtus, the Roman god of bravery and the military, appeared."

I watched him, rapt. He was seeing far into the past now, his gaze on the river.

"He'd been watching me in the arena for years. Apparently he liked my style. He liked how I performed in the revolt even better. A third of my fellow slaves escaped. I would have, too, if I hadn't gone after the emperor."

"You wanted to put a stop to the institution itself, didn't you?"

He nodded. "It's more than one man can do, but I was angry

and foolish. And it's more than the gods would allow. They valued the institution of the Roman Empire."

"Did Virtus stop you?"

"He may have aided the guards, yes. You see, the gods need people to believe in them. The Roman Empire supported that system. The last thing the gods wanted was an overthrow."

"So Virtus smote you?"

A wry grin tugged at the corner of his mouth, and my stomach flip-flopped.

"No. He gave me some of his magic and made me a demigod. I was human before."

My jaw dropped. "A demigod? How?" And no wonder his magic felt so powerful.

"He never liked the gladiator bouts. War is meant to be fought for real, not for play, as far as he was concerned. And he was impressed by my bravery, or something along those lines."

"It was your bravery." It impressed even me, and I didn't want to like him. But I'd seen how many guards there were in his Caipora memory. "And probably the self-sacrifice element, too. I bet gods love that."

"I think they do."

"So how'd you end up here?"

"Well, I was dead. Or almost there. Making me a demigod by giving me some of his power was the only way to bring me back. But obviously I couldn't stay in AD 99. He knew I'd just keep trying to kill the emperor, and that couldn't be allowed. So he sent me forward."

"And you've been here. In the present. That must have been a trip."

He rubbed a hand over his jaw. "There was some...adjusting. Not just to the present day, but to magic. I have powers I never had as a human."

"Swords don't hurt you, and you're a conjuror."

"Very useful. I can conjure anything I need, from money to houses."

"Conjurors can't create money."

"Apparently you can if your power is from a god."

Which made him immeasurably wealthy, though in the brief time I'd known him, he didn't seem into *things.* He wasn't wearing a fancy watch or expensive clothes. "So now you're a demigod living in the modern world. How many years have you been here?"

"Five."

"So that makes you twenty-eight?"

"About. We didn't keep precise track of birthdays, but that's fairly accurate."

"Hmmm. What do you do, now that you're here?"

"Freelance security. Keeps me busy. Right now I'm working for the Order, but I don't always. Sometimes I'm a mercenary, but only for causes I approve of. No drugs or weapons or any of that bullshit that's ruining the earth."

I liked that answer. And it helped that he only occasionally worked for the Order. It gave me hope.

"Now it's your turn." His gaze was intense. Patient.

Dang. I chewed on my lip, debating what to tell him. There weren't many lies that would get me off the hook. And while I was enough of a survivor that I didn't mind lying, I wasn't sure there was anything I could realistically make up.

Ever since the Rebel Gods, trusting was hard for me. It felt like I was pulling out my fingernails to even consider telling him the truth. But there wasn't any other option.

So I went with it and told him about my captivity with the Rebel Gods. The words came slowly at first, painfully and awkwardly. I didn't say why they'd wanted me or that I was supposed to be a Dragon God, but I did mention the new dark magic.

I finished with, "And I have no idea how to get rid of it, but I think the demons know something. The one that I destroyed in The Vaults knew something, at least."

Maximus's dark gaze searched my own. "Then the dark magic isn't yours. I didn't think the signature felt natural. It feels like an ill-fitting costume."

"There's still evil in me." Crap, I shouldn't have said that.

He nodded. "You need to pursue these clues to have any hope of fixing this."

"And I want to stop the murders." They weren't something I could ignore. And with the notes, which I hadn't mentioned to Maximus since I didn't trust him *that* much yet, they felt like they were my responsibility.

"We'll stop them." His voice had turned grim.

I nodded and leaned on the bow, staring out at the moonlit water. There was something up ahead, and I squinted. "Do you see that?"

Maximus leaned forward. "It's a temple, built over the water."

He was right. The massive stone pyramid blocked the river. Unlike Egyptian pyramids, which had smooth sides, this one was made of giant steps leading all the way to the top on all sides. Somehow, the water continued to flow through it, but it definitely looked like we couldn't pass.

I pulled the feather from my bag and touched my tongue to the spot of silver potion that had soaked in, wincing only slightly. Had the owner of this feather come this way? Were we still going the right direction?

An image flashed in my mind of this temple from above. As if the monster had seen it while flying over.

Yes, we were on the right path.

"Hold on!" Eloa shouted. She ran out of the pilothouse and tossed a red rock into the boiler. The steam immediately halted, and the engines stopped pumping. Silence fell, allowing the natural night sounds of the jungle to reign. I hadn't realized how loud the boat was until it stopped.

The vessel drifted slowly toward the temple, and Eloa joined us at the bow.

"Never seen this before." She leaned forward, squinting. "There's got to be a way through."

"You haven't been this way?" I asked.

"Nope. Don't have a death wish. We took a branch of the river that no one is dumb enough to take." She gave me a pointed look. "No one but you."

"Ha-ha." I turned to the pyramid and studied it.

We were close enough now that I could make out carvings on the vertical part of the pyramid's huge steps. They looked ancient, in a style I always associated with a time long past.

I looked at Maximus. "Recognize anything, Grandpa?"

He looked at me, startled. Then choked a laugh. "I'll see what I can do."

He turned back to the temple and studied the images.

The bow of the boat nudged up against the pyramid, and we halted. Water continued to flow around us, but we weren't going to pass unless we figured this out.

The carvings on the massive steps told a story. Something about a man and a journey through the jungle. Not unlike ours, really. In front of each carving was a blackened area, as if a torch had once burned there.

And right in the middle of the pyramid, an area was carved out that was shaped like a huge, ancient spear.

"I think we should put torches in the areas where there are burn marks," I said. "They were once there. Maybe they need to be again."

"All right. I'll do the torches." Maximus raised his hands, and magic flared on the air. The cedar scent of a northern forest filled the humid jungle air, bringing with it the sound of a crashing waterfall.

Eloa watched Maximus with interest as a half dozen torches appeared in his hands. They were lit and everything, which was really quite impressive. Fire was much more difficult to conjure—normally that was the specialty of fire mages.

He climbed out of the boat and onto the pyramid, heading toward the closest illustrated carving that was located roughly in the middle of the pyramid.

"Wait!" I pointed to the left-most carving. "I think the story starts over there. Do that one first."

He then strode over and set the torch into the indent that was carved into the stone. The light illuminated the carving, flickering over the face of the ancient warrior and the monkey that sat on his shoulder.

Both seemed to come alive, moving slightly.

Ted, Eloa's monkey, chattered in delight.

Maximus moved from carving to carving, lighting them up and showing the story of the man as he battled a giant snake and the Caipora.

"He's going on the same journey we are," I said. It was more obvious when the light shined on the images, highlighting previously lost details.

Maximus reached the last one and placed the burning torch. Magic flared on the air, bright and fierce. Light burst from the pyramid, and a massive wind blew out from it, bowling Maximus over.

He fell off the step, managing to grab an edge and avoiding a plunge into the river. Quickly, he yanked himself upright and jumped back onto the boat.

A beam of light shot from the top of the pyramid, going straight into the sky. Then it bent down, shining into the forest like a beacon. It landed somewhere in the woods, probably about fifty yards from shore.

"I think we need to go that way." I looked at Eloa. "Are you going to ditch us if we head over there and check it out?"

She frowned, then shook her head. "As much as I want to, no. I lost that game fair and square, so I'll get you to El Dorado."

I barely repressed a wince. The game hadn't exactly been fair and square. But she had lost, and I wasn't going to tell her any different.

"Thanks." I climbed onto the pyramid and followed Maximus across the lowest step, heading toward the jungle. At the edge, I jumped down onto the spongey ground. We cut through the bushes covered in huge leaves and purple night-blooming orchids. I plucked a few and shoved them in my potions bag.

"Flower collector?" Maximus asked.

"Sort of. For my potions, at least. Rainforest plants are supposed to have all kinds of cool properties."

He cut around the side of a huge tree that soared hundreds of feet in the air, then stopped dead. "I think we've found it."

I edged around him, staring at the massive beam of light that illuminated a golden spear.

"Nice." I hurried to the spear.

"Wait!"

I pulled up short at his voice.

"Let's be careful. Don't touch it yet."

I turned to scowl at him. "Duh."

Though I vibrated with the desire to grab the damned thing, I knelt and inspected it. The weapon was about as tall as I was, and looked like it was made of one hundred percent gold.

I reached into a tiny pocket on my belt and pulled out a minuscule vial.

"What's that?" Maximus asked.

"It'll reveal any latent spells." I uncorked the vial and poured a tiny drop on the spear. The wooden shaft glowed red.

"Some kind of poison or dangerous charm. We shouldn't touch it." I looked around, spotting a huge leaf.

Maximus caught sight of it at the same time, and went to it and yanked it off the stalk, then folded it over itself and used it to pick up the spear.

He strode off through the forest. I followed, climbing up onto the pyramid behind him. He went to the carving of the spear and set the weapon into it. Magic flared again, this time a whirlwind of air that made my hair whip up around my head.

The pyramid began to shake, and I stumbled.

"Hurry!" Eloa shouted.

I leapt onto the boat and went to my knees. Maximus was more graceful, annoyingly.

When I turned, the pyramid had lost half its mass, right in the middle. A tunnel had formed, going straight through the structure, and the space within was pitch black.

I swallowed hard. "That looks inviting."

Eloa barked a laugh and tossed one of the blue rocks into the boiler. "Get ready."

The steamboat surged to life, the engines pumping and the paddlewheel turning. The boat drifted into the darkness.

I walked to the bow and held up my hand, igniting the magic in my light stone ring. It cast a golden glow over the space in front of us, but it wasn't enough to see the interior edges of the tunnel.

"Spooky." Maximus joined me.

"Be alert." Eloa's voice was low. "I feel dark magic here."

She was right. It pricked against my skin. The sound of the engines echoed off the stone walls, exponentially louder. It added to the cocoon-like feeling of the place. This was probably what going back to the womb was like—if your mother was the devil.

I sucked in a steady breath and studied our surroundings. Soon, I spotted a light at the other end. The faintest glow of moonlight on the water, I assumed. We were near the end.

Something rustled against the tunnel wall—like a shifting footstep on stone. My heart leapt into my throat, and I turned, peering into the darkness.

My eyes adjusted in time to see a monster leap from the wall and land on the deck, his footsteps vibrating the metal sheets.

Ah, crap.

8

THE MONSTER WAS MADE OF STONE, A GIANT OF A CREATURE WITH a jaguar's head and a man's body. It raised a huge stone paw tipped with onyx claws.

"Look out!" Eloa shouted. "More coming!"

Maximus conjured a massive mallet and swung for the beast, then smashed it into his chest and bowled him backwards.

Another statue jumped onto the boat from the right side, and I shoved my hand into my bag of potions. The glass bombs had specific shapes as well as colors, and I reached for the triangular one that would disintegrate anything it touched.

The monster lunged for me, its stone monkey jaws open wide. I hurled the potion bomb and dived low, narrowly avoiding having my brains smashed by the creature's claws. I skidded on the metal deck and slammed into the side railing. Pain flared in my shoulder, but I ignored it.

A blast of purple magic flew from the pilothouse, and I spun my head to follow it, watching Eloa's magic blast into another creature. This one had the head of an anaconda that exploded when the magic plowed into it.

"Where've you been hiding *that*?" I shouted as I surged to my feet.

Three more monsters had jumped onto the deck, each with an animal head and human body. Maximus lunged for another stone jaguar and smashed his mallet against the creature's chest, shattering it into a hundred stone shards. Eloa leaned out of the pilothouse and hurled another blast of purple magic at a stone frog man, while I threw a disintegration bomb at a second monkey-headed man.

My potion vial crashed against the creature's leg, which dissolved into dust in seconds. He tumbled over, the rest of his body disintegrating.

The boat chugged out into the open river, leaving the tunnel completely behind. Moonlight lit up the night around us, and I spun, looking for more attackers. The jungle was quiet—relatively speaking. Leaves rustled and monkeys shrieked, but there were no more attackers.

I sighed and leaned against the railing of the boat, catching my breath.

The mallet in Maximus's hand disappeared, and he looked at me. "Are you all right?"

I nodded. "You?"

"That was my idea of a good time." He grinned, and the sight made my insides twist. I couldn't trust him—he worked for the Order—but I wanted to. It was weird, too, because I hadn't trusted anyone except my sisters since my time with the Rebel Gods. Not even the Protectorate people who were my friends. Not really.

To distract myself—and because it was a good idea—I poked into my potions bag to count what I had left. One more disintegration potion, a few paralyzing bombs, a temporary blinding bomb, and the equivalent of a banana peel that a cartoon character would slip on. Not too bad.

I looked up to check the boat's progress, and gasped.

Up ahead, the river curved to the left in a slow and lazy bend. A massive golden wall sat on the edge of the bend in the river, looking like it loomed right in front of us. The thing was huge, a great circular fortress with walls towering high into the darkness of the night. The first morning light reflected off of their smooth surfaces. I'd never been super into gold, but in this context, I could see the appeal.

My awe must have shown on my face, because Maximus turned to look as well.

"Impressive," he murmured.

I turned to Eloa. "Can you drop us off here? Then we can try to sneak up." Maybe a guard had already spotted the boat, but I didn't want to make it extra obvious by chugging up to the front gate.

"I'm going to drop you off and turn around immediately," Eloa said. "I hope you weren't expecting a ride back."

"We'll be fine," Maximus said. "We just needed to find the place. A transport stone will get us out."

"Not if you're within those walls, I bet," Eloa said.

"No, I'm sure you're right." I studied them. Walls that big were meant to keep people out. And in. If a thief managed to sneak in and steal something—a bit like what we were trying to do—they wouldn't want you just transporting out with it. I'd bet a cartload of double chocolate cookies that the place was enchanted to prevent transporting in or out.

"You don't want to come?" I asked Eloa. "Clear your debts with a little bit of that wall."

She scoffed. "You can't take the gold from there, or you'll be cursed. So no, I won't be coming." She turned the boat toward the shore, steering it as close as she dared. "I can't slow down anymore!"

"Thanks!" I shot her a grin, then climbed up onto the railing and jumped onto the shore. I nearly didn't make it, my foot catching at the very edge of the soggy earth, but I got a grip on a vine and pulled myself onto firmer ground.

Maximus, of course, leapt onto it like a giant, muscular gazelle.

I turned and waved at Eloa as she pulled the steamboat around and chugged back down the river. I dusted off my hands and turned to Maximus. "Ready?"

He nodded.

We crept through the forest, silent as ghosts. The leaves rustled around us and jungle creatures shrieked, but I ignored them, focusing instead on the pull of El Dorado. I could almost feel it like a living thing. Maybe that was the dragon in me. Not that I had much, but theoretically, dragons had helped create my kind. Or perhaps it was the call of the feather and my psychometros potion.

We reached the fortress wall, which towered overhead, smooth as glass.

"That will be hard to climb," I whispered.

"There was a gate at the front, but it's too obvious to try to go through there." Maximus conjured a grappling hook, this one with an extremely long rope. He stepped back and swung the thing, launching it high into the sky. The hook caught on the top of the wall.

I craned my head back, swallowing hard. "I really hope that thing doesn't slip off."

"I'll catch you if you fall."

I shot him a sidelong glance. "Pretty hard to do if you're halfway up, too."

He smiled, confidence personified. "I'm quick. But you can go first."

I nodded. There was a time and place to prove my strength.

This wasn't it. I wanted to get in and get my answers without going splat on the jungle floor.

Maximus handed over the rope, and I began to climb, my boots occasionally slipping on the ultra-slick surface of the wall. I vowed that the next potion in my repertoire would be a sticky one that allowed me to climb walls like Spider Man. I grinned at the idea and kept climbing.

By the time I reached the top, my arms ached and my limbs trembled. I flopped onto the flat surface and tried to catch my breath as quietly as I could.

There were no guards on the top of the wall. I guess they expected the giant snake and other monsters to keep people away. Within the walls, everything was made of gold. The morning sun gleamed on a massive fortress that sat on one side. A wide lane led up to it from the main gate, and smaller buildings were scattered around.

Though it looked like it could accommodate thousands, I saw no one on the streets. There was no way we'd be lucky enough that the place was empty and answers were just sitting out for us, but I'd honestly expected more people.

I leaned my head over the edge to watch Maximus ascend. He did so quickly and quietly, racing to the top without issue.

When he appeared at my side, he looked at me. "Not so bad, was it?"

"Could have been worse."

He flipped the rope onto the other side and made sure the hook was anchored, then slid down into the main compound. I followed as quickly as I could, landing on silent feet. We were tucked behind a small building—maybe a house or a shop. Tension thrummed across my skin as I listened for any approach. It was so damned quiet here.

Maximus gripped the rope and flicked his wrist, and the

hook dislodged, plummeting toward us. He caught it, easily avoiding the pointy bits, then made it disappear.

Conjuring was one thing, but making the items that you conjured vanish was even harder. Demigod power wasn't to be taken lightly, that was for sure.

Silently, we edged around the building. There was no one on the narrow street, and the surrounding buildings seemed empty. My heart seemed to thunder in my ears. These people could be allies of the demons and their monster. In fact, they likely were.

"This place is creepy," I murmured.

"It's been a long time since its heyday. But there are people here. The streets are clean, the walls free of vines."

He had a point. Someone worked hard to keep the jungle from devouring this place. But there was an eerie feeling to the air here. Something not quite right. Not entirely dark magic—though there was some of that—but not light magic either.

The only word I could think of was *strange,* and that didn't quite do the trick.

Together, we crept down the quiet street, sticking to the edges of the buildings. Wariness prickled across my skin as we walked, and I realized it was far too silent within the walls of El Dorado. The jungle was so loud that the sound should penetrate even here. Except it didn't.

Why?

When we reached the main central lane that led up to the enormous fortress, I couldn't help but stare in awe. This had to be more than all the gold in the rest of the world put together.

I edged back toward Maximus, not wanting to step away from the cover provided by the building, and murmured, "We should check the back. See if there's a way to sneak in."

He nodded. Before he could speak, a shout sounded.

Crap!

I peeked around the side of the building, looking down the

long lane that led to the main fortress. Two dozen guards stomped toward us. There'd been no one there before.

I lurched backward. "Go!"

I spun to go the opposite direction, hoping to lose myself amongst the narrow lanes and little buildings. Surely there was a nook or cranny we could hide in.

But there were guards there, too, standing right in front of us. My heart jumped into my throat. They had stony expressions, and each wore a long golden cloak. Their swords were the same solid yellow metal and held high, ready to kill.

How the heck had they snuck up on us so quickly and silently? We'd only been standing here for a few seconds. Time had to be slower, or they were unnaturally fast, because we'd *definitely* been alone just moments ago.

I looked behind, and the first group of guards already stood at our backs, having arrived with insane speed.

I shot Maximus a glance, my question clear. Fight or fake it? Because flight wasn't an option—not surrounded on all sides by dozens of guards and solid gold walls.

Maximus stepped forward. "We have come to make a sacrifice to the gods of El Dorado."

Fake it, it was.

Because who the heck were the gods of El Dorado?

The guard in front frowned, his blunt face clearly confused. Maximus just smiled, attempting to look non-threatening. It didn't really work. I'd have to tell him that a guy his size always looked pretty dangerous.

The guard gestured for us to turn around. I did so, hoping that he intended to march us up to the big fortress instead of stab us in the back.

Fortunately, it was the first, less deadly option. The guards fell in around all sides as we marched up. Maximus shot me a glance, and the intent was clear. Keep an eye out for a chance to slip away. We probably wouldn't find one, but right now, it was as likely to work as anything, since we had no idea where to find information about the demons and their monster.

We moved quickly up toward the main fortress, which towered ominously overhead. Sweeping golden stairs gleamed in the light of the morning sun.

We began to climb, our footsteps soundless on the gold. Massive double doors swung open to greet us, and we stepped into a high-ceilinged entranceway that was done entirely in gold.

Honestly, it was all getting to be too much. Clearly no one had told them that gold was more of an accent piece.

"You will meet with the Great One." The lead guard's voice echoed off the walls.

He spoke English? I wouldn't expect that so deep in the jungle, but maybe he recognized that we were foreign.

I shared a glance with Maximus. He gave a pleased little nod. I couldn't help but agree. It was better than the dungeons, and a guy like the Great One would probably have answers.

Whether or not he'd give them to us was another thing altogether.

The guards led us into a similarly decorated room—all gold, natch—where an old man sat on a huge throne. His bronzed skin was heavily creased, with the light from the lanterns gleaming off of it, and his long white hair shined like fresh snow.

The weird feeling that had pervaded the outside of the town was even stronger in here, and it was emanating from the man. I tried to suppress my nerves as we approached. It wouldn't do to show weakness. Or disgust.

The throne was the only thing in the room, and the old man the only living person except for a slender woman who stood against the back wall, her gaze avid with interest. She was much younger than the man, with straight black hair and a gold robe that didn't look natural on her.

In fact, she didn't seem to fit at all. Though she was dressed the part and looked the part, she definitely didn't seem to like it here. A permanent scowl seemed to have dug a line right between her eyes.

"They are here to make a sacrifice," the guard boomed, distracting me from the woman.

Damn. He hadn't forgotten about that. I debated what I would give up, and didn't like my options. I needed my potions for defense, and the knife strapped to my thigh was a gift from my mother. More lucky talisman than anything, but I didn't want to give it up.

Maximus strode forward as if he owned the place, and I hurried to catch up, trying to make my stride look just as confident as his. I wasn't sure I would manage, but damned if I wouldn't try.

The Great One squinted at us, a vaguely annoyed and confused expression on his face. Magic radiated from him, ancient and powerful. I sucked in a shallow breath, trying not to get too deep a whiff. It smelled like a river, and not the fresh kind. His power brought with it the sound of beating drums and the feeling of water surrounding me. I stifled a shudder—it felt a bit like drowning, really, and it sucked. The taste of his magic was a bit moldy, and his aura a pale green.

He had all five signatures, but what *was* he?

Powerful, clearly, but there were no clues as to his magical species.

"You come to make a sacrifice?" Though wispy with age, his voice echoed with power. "For what?"

"We'd like to gain knowledge," Maximus said.

The old man's gaze traveled over us. "Then what will you sacrifice?"

My mind raced. Potions or blade? One was practical, one sentimental.

But which?

I shifted to step forward, but Maximus's hand touched mine lightly. I glanced up. He gave me the most imperceptible shake of his head, then stepped forward, reaching into his pocket.

My heart did a funny little flip.

He was trying to spare me from giving something up.

Maybe I could trust him a little. But he worked for the Order. Indecision warred within me.

When he was only a few feet from the powerful old man, he handed over something tiny. I leaned left to try to see, but couldn't.

"What is it?" the man asked.

"A coin dated to the year AD 98. The last thing that I possess from my past. Very valuable to me, and very valuable historically. It's the only one in existence that hasn't been melted down."

Okay, that was impressive. Though I doubted he could truly know that it was the only one, I liked the spin he put on it.

The man nodded, seeming pleased.

Then he leaned around Maximus and looked at me. "And from you?"

Damn.

At least Maximus had tried.

I stepped forward, my mind racing. When I reached him, I still didn't know what I'd give him. But my hand did. I reached for the pouch of potions at my side. Clearly, my mind was offline and my heart was making the decisions. But I couldn't give up the gift from my mother. It was the only thing I had from her.

I removed the feather and handed over the bag of potions. "It's full of some of my best potions."

Interest lit in the man's eyes. "Potions, you say?"

"You're interested in them?"

"Very."

Hmmm. I stocked that away for later. Maybe we could take a peek in his workshop. Who knew what I could learn from a guy like this. I frowned. Probably some evil shit, now that I thought about it.

He set the offerings on the edge of his seat. "What information do you seek here? What knowledge?"

I held up the feather. "This feather was once here. We'd like to know why."

Understanding gleamed in the man's eyes, and a bit of excitement that made me shiver. His voice trembled with it. "So you've seen it? The monster?"

"Just a glimpse. We're hunting it." Had I given away too much information?

He leaned back. "Ah, now that's a shame. Such beauty should be allowed to fly free."

Uh-oh.

Maximus growled low in his throat. "That beast has killed innocents."

"Beasts must hunt." The man waved his hand, his golden robe fluttering. "It's the nature of the world."

"It's killing too many," I said. "Why was it here? Did it come from here? Did the demons come from here?"

"Neither the demons nor the beast came from here. But they did seek help from me."

"And did you give it?" Maximus asked.

I thought I already knew the answer.

"But of course. Just as I aid you, I aided them."

He probably enjoyed aiding them even more. This guy was too creepy, and so was this place. And the fact that he was spilling his guts to us wasn't a good sign. That's what serial killers did before they killed you, right?

From behind the man, the younger woman watched with interest. I couldn't read anything on her face, but I thought just maybe she disapproved. Then again, that permanent scowl made her look disapproving of everything.

"How did you help it?" I asked.

"The beast is rising and growing stronger. It came here and made an offering in exchange for a potion that would allow it to feed. It had been bound, previously. I fixed that."

Fixed? That wasn't the word I would use.

This man was too in love with the beast and the demons that were using it for their evil deeds. There was no way he'd just tell us how to stop it. It was clear now that we'd have to find that out on our own. And also manage to not get killed by his guards.

I glanced at Maximus, trying to convey this with my eyes, but he was already speaking.

"I understand your perspective, Great One." He was clearly trying to sound impressed by the old man's logic, and it almost worked. If I hadn't known how badly he wanted to stop the creature, I might have believed him. "You are enlightening me."

Oh, he was full of it.

The old man nodded, clearly pleased. Ego was getting in his way. "I'm glad you see reason."

"I most definitely do." Maximus's shoulders dropped so slightly I almost didn't notice. As if he were tired. "We are exhausted after our long journey. Is there a place we might rest and take respite?"

"But of course." A shifty gleam entered the old man's eyes. He waved his hand, which I noticed were tipped with golden claws, and the guards behind us stomped to attention. "They will show you the way."

I nodded my thanks, then turned to accompany the guards. Would we run for it now, or hope that we actually were being shown to a private place to rest? It'd be better to sneak out than break out, and Maximus clearly agreed, because he followed the guards without argument.

It was as we were going down our fourth flight of stairs that I started to get nervous. Wasn't the bottom floor where they always kept the dungeons?

It totally was.

I hoped El Dorado would be different, but somehow, I doubted it. I glanced at Maximus, and from the tightness to his brow, he seemed to agree that something was up.

His gaze met mine and his mouth moved silently. "Run left."

I jerked my head, then turned to the left and made to sprint. The guards were fast, though, wickedly so. They stepped right in front of me, boxing me in. Others fell in line behind. They even managed to stop Maximus.

Then they closed in, squeezing us tight, and marched on. It was almost as if they picked us up and carried us with them. My heart thundered and my skin chilled.

We'd lost all control.

We flowed on at their unnatural speed, and before I knew it, I'd been shoved into a pit.

The ground disappeared, and the wind tore at my hair as I fell, a scream trapped in my throat.

9

THE SCREAM FINALLY BROKE FREE, ECHOING IN THE DARK AS I plummeted toward certain death.

Maximus fell beside me, stoically quiet. His magic flared on the air, bringing with it the welcome scent of cedar and the sound of a waterfall that managed to buffer some of my screams.

Please be saving us!

Because even if I had my magic, there was nothing I could do to save us from going splat.

Then I landed.

And bounced.

Whatever I'd fallen on had been full of air, bouncing me back up through the tunnel. I fell again, and bounced again, repeating the routine several times until I lay still, staring up at the light above, my head spinning and my breath heaving.

We'd fallen down a narrow circular shaft that was at least a hundred feet deep. It'd felt longer, actually. I wasn't entirely sure that the individuals here didn't screw with time, somehow. Between the swiftness of the guards and the long drop, time seemed to flow abnormally in El Dorado.

My breath heaved and my adrenaline faded, making my limbs shake. I was lying on some kind of huge air mattress that filled the whole bottom of the shaft. Maximus lay next to me.

"Well done," I said. "A bit cartoonish, but it worked."

"I saw it on television once." He sounded a bit dazed.

"Watch a lot of TV, do you?"

"No. But when I first arrived from the past, it did help."

"I can imagine." Trembling, I sat. The walls that surrounded us were made of pure gold, so smooth that there was no way we could climb out.

Beneath me, the air mattress began to deflate. As we slowly sank down to the ground, I looked at Maximus. "Thanks for making a sacrifice so I didn't have to."

"Didn't work."

"But you tried." I hardly knew the guy. Why had he done that? To lure me into trusting him? "Was that really the last thing you owned from your past?"

He nodded. "I had it on me when I was turned into a demigod and brought forward through time. But it was time to let go of the past, anyway."

Let go of the past.

What a fantastic idea. I'd tried it, of course. I'd made an effort to put my captivity behind me and forget all the bad. The problem was that the mind wasn't so easy. When I was asleep, or weak, or sick, or just feeling out of sorts, the terrible memories would rise again.

The cushion deflated entirely, and my butt hit the hard surface of the ground.

Maximus made the air mattress disappear entirely and stood. "I have a transport charm but it'd be a waste. This pit will be protected against transporting, no doubt."

I agreed. "How about a giant ladder."

"Exactly what I was thinking." He squinted upward. "Though there are now bars at the top of our cage."

"I might have something that can melt through that."

"You gave away your potions."

I tapped my belt. "Not all of them."

"Let's move quickly, then. It sounds like the demons are creating some kind of super killer, and we need to figure out how to stop it from feeding."

"I'm thinking we try to counteract whatever magic the old man gave the bird. So we need to hit up his workshop and see what we can find. If we know what he used, maybe we can make something to counter it."

He flashed a quick smile. "I love having a plan."

"That's how you did so well in the gladiator ring, isn't it?"

He nodded, his gaze shuttering, and suddenly I felt a bit shitty. He had a tough, cool past, if one looked at it from the outside. Badass gladiator, king of the ring.

But in reality, he'd been forced to fight for his life. Forced to kill others to survive. It had to have been horrible. So horrible that he'd *died* trying to end the institution itself. If he hadn't been so brave and freaking strong, the god Virtus wouldn't have blessed him with his power, and he'd just be dust.

"Sorry," I said.

He shook his head. "It's nothing."

"It's not. But we can pretend it is."

Another small smile quirked the side of his mouth, then his magic flared on the air. A ridiculously long ladder leaned against the side of the pit, leading all the way to the top. Maximus climbed on, moving quickly upward. I followed, doing my best to keep up, but my legs were still shaky from the fall.

When I reached the top, it was obvious that the metal bars were too narrow to slip through. Maximus pushed at them, his biceps bulging, but they didn't move. He pushed harder. The ladder began to creak.

"Stop!" I hissed.

He was pushing so hard that the ladder was breaking. Dude was strong.

I dug into the potion belt and pulled out a tiny vial of highly concentrated disintegration potion. It was smaller than my pinky, but full of enough liquid to make gallons if I could dilute it with water.

I had a feeling we'd need the full strength, though.

"Here, take this," I whispered, passing up the tiny vial. "Don't let it touch your skin."

I held my breath as he uncorked it, then reached out and dripped a tiny bit onto the top of one of the bars. That was it. The metal should smoke and disintegrate. Right about now.

Now.

Now?

Nope.

It didn't work.

I scowled. "Dump the rest."

He did, but that didn't work either.

I sagged. Shit.

"Nothing will work," a feminine voice said, speaking in a slight accent. "It's enchanted."

I looked up, spying the familiar face of the woman who'd stood sentry in the Great One's hall. Her scowl had faded slightly, the deep crease between her eyes gone.

"I don't suppose you're here to help us?" I asked.

She shrugged, an elegant motion. "I could be. Will you take me with you when you leave? Get me out of this damned jungle?"

"Sure." That was an easy agreement to make. We could fit three through the transport charm's portal if we ever made it outside the walls of El Dorado to use the thing. "But how can we trust you?"

"I don't think you have any other option."

Maximus looked down at me. "She has a point."

Though I was loath to trust any stranger, they were both right. We were up shit creek, and she might have a paddle.

"I can also tell you something you desperately want to know." She looked right at me.

"How do you know what I want to know?"

"I can see it in you."

"You're a seer?" I asked, hope fluttering in my chest. "Prove it."

"I'm a good one. Locked away here, though. But I know about the dark magic in your soul. It's connected to the demons and monster that came here."

"How?"

"I don't know how or why, but every time they feed, the dark magic in you grows stronger. They give off a magical energy when they kill and eat. It makes them stronger, and somehow, it's igniting the dark magic in you, too."

"Holy fates." That explained why it was suddenly bursting to the surface. The dark power had been with me since the Rebel Gods, and now it was coming to the surface because the demons' monster was rising.

Was *it* connected to the Rebel Gods?

I shivered, clinging to the ladder. It shouldn't be. The Rebel Gods were *dead.* But this was hard to ignore.

A new horrible thought rose. What if they killed every time that the magic burst out of me? What if *I* caused this, not the other way around? The magic helped me—though it was dark, it had saved my life. What if it led to the death of another?

Panic flared. "How do I get rid of the magic?"

"I don't know how to get *rid* of it. But if you can stop them from feeding, the magic will stop growing. Before the monster came to my uncle, its beak and claws had been bound by magic. It could not pierce flesh. My uncle gave it a potion to counteract that and to make the beast stronger."

Of course. As I'd suspected. "So if we can make another potion or find the proper spell, we could undo your uncle's work. They could no longer feed. And maybe weaken it enough to kill it."

"Exactly. You'd need a counterspell. My uncle's work is so powerful that you can't fight the beast as long as it is protected by his potion."

Maximus looked down at me. "We need to go. Now."

I nodded, looking at her. "Get us out of here, and we're you're one-way ticket out of crazy town."

She grinned, her white teeth flashing, and held her palm over the grate. Magic popped on the air, feeling like a rubber band snapping against my skin.

"Old bugger trusts me," she muttered. "Moron. Keeps me locked up and assumes I'm happy here. Ha."

"Can't see past his own ego, I bet," I said.

Her gaze met mine. "Exactly. Everyone kowtows to him so he assumes it's normal. It's not."

"Definitely not." I'd have agreed with her on pretty much any topic to get her to open that gate, but I did actually agree with her on that. Some folks held power for so long that they forgot what it was to be a real person. Considering that this dude went by the name Great One, his perspective was totally screwed.

She removed her hand. "There. The spell is broken."

Maximus pushed on the gate and it rose. He was agile as he slipped out while still holding it up, then he stood and lifted it farther. I scrambled out as if there were a fire behind me and stood.

Maximus lowered the grate, and I turned to the woman, holding out my hand. "I'm Rowan."

"I'm Zoana, great niece of the Great One. Small 'g' for me, though."

I grinned. "Can you show us where his workshop is? I need a sample of whatever he gave the monster."

She blanched, hesitating. Clearly she'd rather just run for it.

"You know its value to Rowan. We have to have it," Maximus said. "Can't leave without it."

She chewed her lip, fiddling with her golden robe. Then she huffed and nodded. "But we'll need to be quick. I only have so much magic, and we'll need a lot of it to control the guards."

"So they *are* extra fast."

"They can be."

"Then let's move," Maximus said.

On swift, silent feet, Zoana led us up four flights of stairs and down several winding halls. We continued to go up, moving faster as we went. It was as if panic drove Zoana, and I couldn't blame her. The whole time we'd been here, I'd seen nothing but plain gold walls, floor, pit, and one throne. There was nothing here but gold, and it was boring as hell. No wonder she wanted out.

"Almost there," she whispered.

We rounded a corner and came to a door. A guard stood there, his face bored. As soon as he saw us, his brows jumped and his mouth opened as if to shout.

Zoana threw out her hand and whispered, "Sleep!"

He collapsed, keeling over like a redwood and then slamming to the ground, where he began to snore vigorously.

"Wow," I murmured. "Mind control?"

"A little bit. I can't do very much. You need to hurry." She waved to the door.

I moved toward it and slipped inside. The first thing I saw was Romeo the raccoon, sitting on a table lined with jars.

"What the hell are you doing here?" I hissed.

Poppy and Eloise sat next to him, riffling through the various jars.

I could sense you needed help. But then we got a bit…distracted. This is the only thing in this whole place that isn't made of gold.

Poppy hissed.

I know, Poppy. Still not trash.

I could not believe these guys. They were supposed to be my helpful sidekicks, but they got distracted by the promise of trash?

"These are your friends?" Zoana asked.

I turned to look at them, catching the quizzical expression on Maximus's face. "Yeah, you could put it that way."

I turned back to Romeo, who was grinning broadly, his pointy white fangs gleaming. *Friends.*

"Yeah, get over it."

He nodded, then pointed to a collection of jars at the side. *Those smell like the feather we gave you.*

I grinned at him. "Well done, you."

He tapped his nose. *Got a good sniffer.*

The badger grumbled.

Not as good as you, Eloise. He looked at me. *It's true. Eloise sniffed it first.*

My life was officially nuts. But if it worked, it worked. I hurried to the jars. "The Menacing Menagerie says that this smells like the feather. They're probably the ingredients for the potion." I picked one up and unscrewed it, taking a whiff. I couldn't exactly place it, but it did smell familiar.

"He was just using those recently," Zoana said.

"Good enough for me." I tumbled them all into a bag that I

found on another table, then looked at Maximus, who was sorting through a few more.

He grabbed a few, then handed them over to me. "Let's get out of here."

I looked at the Menagerie. "You good to get home?"

We got it, boss.

I nodded, then turned to Zoana. "Let's go."

She grinned, then turned and raced from the room, heading down the stairs.

I hurried to catch up. "We just need to get outside the main compound wall to use our transport charm, unless you know a space inside that doesn't block transport magic."

"No, we definitely need to be outside the walls for that. The whole place is blocked. No transporting in or out."

As I'd thought.

We raced through the halls on silent feet. This was going too smoothly. The sun was fully overhead when we made it out of the main building. It shined so brightly on the gold that it was nearly blinding.

"Come on!" Zoana waved us forward. "There's a back gate over here."

As soon as she'd spoken, the guards appeared. Over two dozen of them, so fast that I hadn't even heard them coming. They closed in, surrounding us.

Maximus conjured a sword and lunged, moving so quickly I almost couldn't see him. He'd beheaded four guards within seconds.

Holy fates.

I'd never seen anyone fight like him.

Zoana threw out her hands, hissing, "Sleep!"

Two of the guards keeled right over.

I ignored the dagger at my thigh—too small—and dragged a sword from the ether, wishing that I had my potion bombs.

I swung for the nearest guard and sliced him across the chest. He bellowed and stumbled back. Another darted toward me, sweeping out with his blade. I ducked, jabbing upward with mine and sinking it into his gut.

To my left, Maximus was a whirlwind. Blood sprayed, but he was so quick that a drop never landed on him. I could see how he'd survived so long in the fighting pits.

When a guard's blade sliced toward his arm, Maximus didn't even flinch. No wound, either, just like before.

But there were so many guards. They seemed to be appearing out of nowhere.

Panic flashed on Zoana's face. "They won't stop coming!"

"Eventually, they have to." I panted as I swung my sword, trying to ignore the pain of a recent slice to my thigh.

"No, they don't." Her gaze met mine. "My great uncle's magic is powerful."

The fear in her eyes made my heart thunder. Crap, she was really afraid. And it made me believe her. The guards might never stop coming.

I kept fighting, but she was right. More and more came. Even Maximus couldn't take them all on—not if they were endless in number.

Panic rose in my chest.

Trapped. I was trapped here, fighting endless guards with golden swords.

It was the same feeling I'd had with the Rebel Gods, and the same feeling with the demon in The Vaults. The same feeling with the Caipora.

Trapped. Doomed.

When the dark magic started to rise in my belly, I expected it. The darkness came whenever I felt like I was going to die. Whenever I felt as trapped as I had been with my captors for five years.

I fought it, desperately not wanting to give in to the evil. It tainted my soul, made sickness sweep through my limbs.

But I couldn't fight it. It was too strong.

My eyes began to glow. I could only tell because the faces of the men in front of me gleamed even brighter than they had before.

Oh, crap.

We really needed any help we could get right now—and my dark magic sure packed a hell of a punch—but I didn't want it to escape. Not again.

I had no choice, though. It was like a steam train barreling down.

"Zoana, Maximus. Get down!"

Their gazes flashed to me, shock evident. The fear in my voice was so strong that they reacted immediately. They dived low, scrambling away through the legs of the guards. The movement shocked the hell out of the guards, who couldn't figure it out for a few seconds.

It gave Zoana and Maximus just enough time to get far enough away. I hoped. Because I was out of control. The power had filled me up to the brim. It made my skin feel like it would burst from the pressure.

The magic exploded out of me, darkness blasting the guards into dust.

Frantic, I searched for Zoana and Maximus. They were huddled on the ground, covered in the remains of the guards.

Ew.

"Come on!" I said. More guards would come, but hopefully I'd bought us a bit of time.

My friends leapt up. Zoana's bright eyes met mine. Then she turned, sprinted toward the gate, and pressed her hand to it. The latch sparked with magic, then the gate swung open. We darted out into the jungle.

Behind us, guards shouted.

"Hurry!" I yelled to Maximus.

He shoved his hand into his pocket and withdrew the transportation charm, then hurled it to the ground. A cloud of glittery gray smoke rose upward, and I grabbed Zoana's hand, lunging into it.

The last thing I heard was the roar of the guards, and I prayed the portal would close before they could reach it.

10

I ARRIVED IN THE GRASSMARKET, PANTING. MAXIMUS APPEARED next to us, and the portal closed behind him. No guards followed, thank fates.

I looked at Zoana. "Are you okay?"

She nodded, her face pale. "I never thought I'd escape that jungle."

I frowned. "You were able to walk right out of the gate, though."

"Yes, but how was I going to get through the jungle on foot? Without a boat, it's a two month walk. With no food or fresh water and monsters at every turn?"

"Right. Them." In all the stress and adventure, I'd forgotten about them. But honestly, giant monsters were such a normal part of my everyday that I hadn't registered them as a real issue.

"Well, thank you." She nodded at us both. "I'll be on my way."

"Wait, you've been in the jungle all your life. Don't you need help, like, assimilating?" I waved my hands to gesture to everything around us.

She looked around, her eyes wide. "It *is* different. But I'll be fine. If my uncle comes after you for taking his potions, I don't want to be anywhere near you."

"Fair enough," Maximus said. "But if you need help, the Undercover Protectorate can hide you."

I nodded. "They protected my sisters when they were running from something terrible."

"I'll keep it in mind." She smiled. "But someone has been in control of me my whole life. I want to be in control now."

With that, she slipped away into the crowd.

I looked at Maximus. "Thank fates for her."

He nodded. "Let's take the portal back to the Protectorate."

I followed him through the busy streets, passing by supernaturals of all varieties. Dusk was falling and shop windows were lighting up, sending a golden glow over the cobblestones and storefronts.

Maximus seemed to know exactly where the portal to the Protectorate was located, and I followed his longer strides toward the alley.

"You're allowed to go through the portal?" I asked. "I thought only Protectorate members could."

"Jude gave me special permission."

"Ah. Because you're training me." I followed him into the alley.

He turned abruptly and faced me, looming in the dark. I startled a bit, then held my ground.

"Speaking of that." His voice was low. "I wanted to wait until we were away from the crowds. But your dark magic went haywire back in the jungle."

I swallowed hard. "I know."

"And your skin now has a gray cast to it."

My hand flew to my cheek. "Wait, what? Gray?"

He nodded, his brows lowered and his mouth flat. "The dark magic is growing inside you. I think the signature is manifesting as a gray aura. You're going to have to learn to control your signature to keep anyone from knowing what is happening. And if you can't control the magic, I can't guarantee you won't be discovered. I should turn you in, but..."

He looked like maybe he didn't want to. *Please don't want to.*

"Just try harder to control your power. You have to."

Shit, shit, shit. "I don't know how to do that."

"I can help you with learning to repress your signature, but it's just a Band-Aid. We're going to have to find the counterspell to whatever the Great One gave the monster. Once we've stopped it from feeding, you'll hopefully have a break and be able to get the magic under control."

I nodded, my heart pounding. Was he really going to help me with this? Since he was a member of the Order, it was his job to toss me in the Prison for Magical Miscreants, but he'd also been hired by the Protectorate to help me. But he seemed torn, almost. Or maybe that was wishful thinking.

"Let's get back to the Protectorate and see what the others have found out. I'm pretty good with potions, but Hedy is a genius with this kind of thing."

"Hedy?"

"The R&D witch. She develops new spells and weapons for us. Like Q from James Bond."

He grinned. "I've seen that one. She must be useful."

"Very."

We hurried to the portal and stepped through. Again, there was the briefest hesitation. The magic in the portal was starting to sense the darkness in me. It didn't want to let me through to the Protectorate in case I was a threat.

Dread filled me, dark and thick.

Finally, the portal spat me out into the enchanted glen. I did my best to shake away the dread. Fairy lights twinkled through the gnarled old trees, lighting the way down the path. It didn't take long to reach the main lawn, and we raced up the castle steps. As always, the massive wooden doors swung open to permit us entrance to the huge hall.

As if she'd seen us coming across the grass, Jude raced down the main stairs, her starry blue eyes glued to us. "Well? What did you find?"

"A definite clue," I said. "Can we get Hedy in the round room? Lachlan, too, if he's around."

Lachlan was Ana's boyfriend. He was a master potion maker and the Arch Magus, the most powerful mage in the world. Between him and Hedy, they could figure this out. Though I was getting pretty danged good with potions, I'd only been at it six months. They'd been practicing for years. I'd learned a lot from both of them, in fact.

"I'll find them." She turned to head back up the stairs, then stopped and turned back around, squinting at me. "Are you all right? You look a bit ill."

I swallowed hard. "Um, just a rough trip through the jungle."

"Ah." She nodded knowingly, but I was pretty sure she didn't realize what was wrong with me.

She turned and I shared a glance with Maximus. He was willing to keep my secret now, but for how long?

I looked at him, but his expression was unreadable. I started toward the round room.

Maximus followed me down the ancient hall, past old artwork and flickering sconces. A huge round table was set up in the round room, and I felt a bit like Arthur and his knights as I sat.

A few moments later, the rest joined us. Hedy and Jude sat

on the other side of the table, while Lachlan and Bree took a spot between us. Lachlan was a tall, dark-haired man with dark eyes and a strong aura of power. In a way, he was a bit like Maximus.

They introduced themselves, then Jude leaned forward. "What did you find?"

I put the pouch of the Great One's potions on the table and pushed it across, then told the story of our adventure in the jungle.

"That's good stuff," Jude said.

"We can definitely make progress with this." Hedy dug into the bag and removed the ingredients. She passed some over to Lachlan, who inspected them.

"What has everyone else found?" I asked.

"Ali and Haris might have a lead on the demons' current location, so they are tracking that," Jude said. "Ana and Caro are off trying to find out what kind of bird or beast has a feather like the ones left at the scene. There've been two more murders, but no one from the PITs arrived in time to catch the monster."

"There will be even more," Maximus said. "The demons are creating a super monster and letting it loose. Every time it feeds, it grows stronger. There's no reason for them to stop."

Hedy and Lachlan stood.

Hedy looked at Jude. "We'll get started right away on analyzing these ingredients. Hopefully we'll find a counterspell soon, and the beast will no longer be able to break flesh with its claws and beak."

Lachlan looked at me. "Rowan, do you want to be part of this? I know you're interested in potions."

Interested was one way to put it. Developing the potions had become my lifeline—something I was good at when I had no other magic.

"I don't know." Bree frowned. "Maybe Rowan should rest. She doesn't look well."

I barely resisted touching my cheek. I needed to get this dark magic under control. At least enough to control my signature so it didn't turn my skin gray and make me look like death. "I don't feel that bad. Maximus was going to show me a few fight moves, then I'll join you in Hedy's workshop."

Jude smiled. "Good. I'm glad you're taking your training seriously. You're going to need it if you want to pass the Academy."

Jude was a hard taskmaster, but I appreciated it. I nodded.

We split up, and I met Maximus at the door. "I'm going to grab a quick shower and change of clothes. Where do you want to do the training?"

"Outside is fine. Away from people."

I nodded, then left him. He wasn't living in the castle, so did he have a place to get cleaned up? Should I invite him up to mine?

No.

I didn't want to get too attached. I needed to focus on my work, and attachments were dangerous. Especially to an Order of the Magica person. I couldn't trust him. Not as long as he worked for them.

I shoved away thoughts of Maximus and hurried up to my apartment. The halls were quiet as I slipped through, and I was grateful not to run into anyone. It had been obvious Bree wanted to ask me questions about the gray cast to my skin, but Jude had asked her to go on a job, so she'd departed.

My touch unlocked the door to my tower apartment, and I climbed the stairs to the main floor. I pushed open the door, my shoulders relaxing at the sight of my own space. It might be cluttered and full of potions and equipment, but it was mine.

A rustling from the kitchen on the left made me stiffen. It

was open to the main living space, with a low butcher block bar separating it from the living room, but I could see no one.

Carefully, I drew a sword from the ether. "Who's there?"

I edged toward the kitchen, every surface of which was covered with potion-making stuff and a few packages of double chocolate cookies. My skin tightened as I waited for the intruder to show themselves. But no one did.

I stepped in and spotted the cabinet door to the trash swinging open. At that moment, the trash bin tumbled over, and three creatures rolled out of it.

Romeo blinked up at me, then grinned, his little fangs sharp and white.

Poppy had an old cheese rind in her paws, and Eloise the badger had a yogurt cup. They'd bypassed the cookies entirely and went straight for the trash bin. To each their own.

Hello, friend. Romeo grinned wider.

"What the hell are you doing here?"

You said we could have your trash. He plucked dejectedly at an empty beer bottle. *But there's not quite as much as I'd hoped.*

"I'm just one person."

Well, you could eat at home more. His eyes brightened at that. *If you don't eat here, you must eat somewhere else in this palatial estate.*

"Palatial estate? What kind of raccoon says that?"

He brushed off his shoulder and gave me a sassy look. *Smart raccoons.* He nudged Poppy and Eloise with his foot. *Come on. We're off to find better trash.*

Poppy nodded, as if saying *About time.*

She was a bit of a grumpy possum, but I liked her. Eloise was more of the strong and silent type, but I liked her, too.

They hurried off, and I grabbed a cookie, chowing down. Still chewing, I hopped into the shower, cleaning up as quickly as I could. While the water pounded on me, I focused on the dark magic that filled me up. It made me feel vaguely ill, a slight nausea that was off-putting. I sucked in a slow breath and tried to force the magic back down, driving it deep inside myself so the gray cast would leave my skin.

Every time I thought I had a handle on it, it slipped through my grasp.

Damn it.

I needed to get control of this, but I couldn't. I freaking hated magic at this point. The Rebel Gods had forced me to use it against my sisters, which any good shrink would say had given me PTSD or an aversion to magic or something like that, but I wanted to be stronger. I wanted to fight my way past this.

But I just *couldn't.*

Tears smarted my eyes, and I blinked them back, determined not to let them fall.

I shut off the water and got out, drying off quickly and then switching out my clothes. Pink and black again, with neon-green underwear that featured a giraffe's head on the butt. Goofy underwear was a weakness of mine, along with my pink lipstick and weird, fancy beer. No one would see it, but that wasn't the point. Then I refilled my potions belt and strapped my mother's dagger to my leg. After grabbing my bag of potions, I headed back down the stairs. Before going outside, I swung by the kitchens beneath the main hall.

As usual, Hans was bustling around, his white chef's hat crooked on his head. Boris the rat rode on top, his constant companion. Once upon a time, I might have been grossed out by a rat in the kitchen.

After my captivity, however, when things had been *really* bad, I found it charming. Life was too short to be bothered by rats. And Boris had some truly excellent hygiene, always washing his little hands in the sink but making a point to stay away from the food, for the most part.

"You brought guests!" Hans's mustache quivered with delight as he pointed to my three new sidekicks.

Romeo, Poppy, and Eloise were set up at a small table near the fire, each dining on a plate of trash.

"They insisted on only eating from the bin." Hans grinned. "Such a brilliant way to reduce waste."

The Menacing Menagerie shot me three fangy smiles. I gazed back at them, bemused, then asked Hans for a couple of sandwiches.

He handed them over, along with two juice boxes. "Don't forget your juice!"

He had a thing for juice.

I'll eat your crusts if you don't want them.

"Finish your plate first, Romeo. Looks like you've got some good garbage on there."

Do I!

I left them to it, eating my sandwich as I hurried up the stairs. I found Maximus waiting for me at the main exit, and I handed him the second sandwich.

"Thank you."

"There's a juice box where that came from."

"Juice box?" He frowned.

I handed him the box of grape juice, and his expression cleared.

"Ah, those. I've seen them on the television. For children."

"Or for powerful supernaturals." I stuck a straw in and sucked, not bothering to explain Hans's strange obsession. "This is one of the first modern things you've had trouble with. How are you so well assimilated?"

"A lot of practice. We'll go over there, toward the woods." Maximus led the way, eating his sandwich as we walked.

Once we arrived, he took my discarded juice box and made it

disappear, along with his own trash. Had the Menagerie been here, I'm sure they would have liked that trash.

"Handy."

"Very." He stepped back. "Have you tried controlling your magic at all?"

"Of course. But I can't get a handle on it. I focus as hard as I can, and as soon as I think I have a grip on it, it disappears."

He nodded. "That's your problem. It's counterintuitive, but you need to not try so hard."

I scowled, hating the sound of that.

"It's the problem of the white bear. When you try not to think of a white bear, all you can do is think of a white bear. It comes into your mind no matter what."

"Okay, that makes some sense. So what do I do?"

He conjured two blunt wooden swords, and tossed me one. "Practice while distracted." He swung his sword loosely. "We'll spar, and you try to loosely hold on to your magic. Envision it as a ball in your free hand. Squeeze it to force it down, but keep your mind on the fight."

"Like a stress ball?"

"I don't know what that is, but sure."

I grinned. A second modern day slipup. It was so easy to forget that he'd only spent five years in present day.

"Now, go." He moved toward me, swinging his sword.

He was clearly pulling his punches, moving slower than he normally would, and I wasn't freaking having it. I lunged and slammed my wooden blade against his. They smashed together, the vibration rising up my arm.

His brows rose. "You're quick."

"I'm good." I parried, then swung again, going for his waist. All the while, I squeezed my hand, occasionally envisioning sending my magic back down, deep inside me.

He dodged the blow, spinning around, then struck out with his blade and tapped me on the arm.

Annoyance flared. Slight nausea followed.

"Get ahold of your magic," he said. "Don't let your emotions allow you to lose control."

I gritted my teeth, but he was right. The annoyance *did* make me lose control. I sucked in a breath as I dodged his blow, steadying my mind and gripping my fist tight.

Somehow, it worked. The fight kept my mind distracted enough and somehow helped me control the dark magic. I felt better as I fought, the darkness clearly receding inside me.

Sweat began to form on my skin, warmth flowing over me. We fought in the moonlight, and he was so skilled that it took everything I had to keep up.

I dodged one blow and managed to hit him in the leg with my blade, but he was quick, too, delivering his own strike to my shoulder.

We danced—there was no other word for it. It was violent and fast, but it was a dance all the same.

I preferred this to any nightclub. My mind felt free as I fought, and my magic stayed mostly under control. I couldn't keep my eyes off his muscles though. Or his movements. He fought with such grace that it was mesmerizing.

Actually, I became a little warm, just watching him. The tension between us was tight as a wire, and it was far from violent. My breath came quicker, not just from the workout.

I couldn't stop looking at his mouth.

Annoyed with myself, I picked up the intensity, moving forward.

He blocked my next blow, and I lunged forward, striking again. His arm came up, and he grabbed my wrist, stopping my sword in midair.

I breathed hard, so close to him that I could smell the scent of his sweat. It was...nice. Manly and sexy, somehow. My breath caught in my throat as my gaze dropped to his mouth.

I licked my lips, unable to help myself.

His gaze dropped, following the motion, and heat rose in his eyes.

I want to kiss him.

My breath heaved in my lungs, and I tried to control it. I moved closer to him, unable to help myself. His gaze darkened, turning molten.

11

"They've found something!" The voice echoed across the lawn, high and excited.

Maximus and I jerked apart.

Heat rose in my cheeks, and I turned to face the castle. Florian, the ghostly librarian, was running down the lawn. The Pugs of Destruction followed behind him, their ghostly forms glowing in the moonlight. Mayhem led the trio, her little wings keeping her aloft. Ruckus and Chaos followed, springing across the lawn. Chaos's horns rose tall off his head, while Ruckus's fangs hung over his little lower lip.

They were ridiculous, but had been an institution at the Protectorate for years. They were Bree's sidekicks when they weren't hanging out with Florian in the library.

He came to a halt in front of us, panting. His pale eyes were bright. "Hedy sent me to find you. They think they have a clue."

"Excellent." I turned to Maximus. "How do I look?"

"Not gray."

"Great. Good enough for me."

Florian's gaze darted between us, clearly sensing that something was up, but he said nothing.

"Let's go see what they've found." I turned and hurried off toward Hedy's workshop, which was located near the main gate in the castle's exterior curtain wall. She kept it away from the castle in case something blew up. I thought it was good policy and should probably get a place like that myself.

The round tower's door was open as we approached, light glowing from within.

I stepped inside, spotting Hedy and Lachlan bent over a table. They looked up.

"Good, you're here." Hedy's eyes brightened. "I'm surprised you wanted to miss this, though you do look better."

I hadn't wanted to miss it, but I didn't dare say that for fear I'd have to explain. "What did you find?"

She pointed to a bowl, which was filled with a gleaming silver liquid. Next to it lay one of the beast's feathers. "We've recreated it. It's a revival potion. Ancient in origin. Definitely from a jungle. I don't know what it's called exactly, but I was able to recreate what was on the feather."

"Is there a counterpotion or spell?"

"According to this book, there is." She pressed her finger to the ancient leather-bound tome on the table. If we throw it on the beast, it will bind it and keep it from attacking. It can still menace people, but it won't be able to tear them apart with its beak and claws."

"And most importantly," Lachlan said, "it won't be able to feed and grow stronger."

I nearly sagged with relief. That was exactly what I wanted to hear.

"Exactly," Hedy said. "And the counterspell will make it possible to kill the beast. Right now, with this potion coating its feathers, it's nearly indestructible. Their feathers will repel other potions, and their beak and claws are deadly. But the counterspell potion should weaken it enough that you can kill it."

"So we definitely need this counterspell potion," I said.

"I don't think you stand a chance without it," Hedy said. "It'd be impossible to kill them."

"Can you make it?" Maximus asked.

"That's the tricky part. This book doesn't have the exact recipe, and I've not yet figured it out. I think it's because I may not have all the ingredients."

"I can go ask Connor in Magic's Bend," I said, referring to our mutual friend who was a potions whiz.

Hedy nodded. "That would be good. We'll keep working on it, too. Whoever figures it out first will alert the others."

"And we need to find where the beast is hiding."

"The rest of the PITs are searching for them," I said.

Maximus frowned. "The PITs?"

"The Paranormal Investigative Team," Hedy said. "Led by Jude. Though the acronym is a bit funny."

"Ah, right. I recall." He looked at me. "I'll accompany you to Magic's Bend."

"Let's leave now."

"Murder!" The shout sounded from outside.

Everyone jerked and whirled toward the door. Florian stumbled in, his eyes wild. "There's been another one. In the Grassmarket."

"Holy fates," Hedy said. "Again?"

"Again." He shook his head. "I'm doing this too much lately, bursting into rooms and shouting murder."

Dread welled within me.

No.

Not another. We were failing at every turn. The murders kept piling up, and we were too slow.

Jude caught my eye. "Will you stop by the scene and use your psychometros potion on any clues there might be?"

I swallowed hard, but nodded. I didn't want to see the scene, but I had to.

"First, take this." Hedy scooped up tiny vials of liquid, then handed me a piece of paper that looked like it had ingredients written on it, along with a copy of one of the book's pages. "That's all my notes and samples of the stuff you took from El Dorado. I've done my best, and hopefully Connor can take it from here and figure out how to make the counterspell. His ingredient collection is impressive, so that should help." She shook her head. "I like to think I'm the best, but sometimes you need teamwork."

After being alone with the Rebel Gods for so long, that was one of my favorite things about the Protectorate. We worked together, and when we couldn't figure something out, we had other friends to help us.

I took the things from her and shoved them in the pockets of my leather jacket, then zipped them up, turned, and hurried from her workshop.

It didn't take Maximus, Lachlan, and me long to reach the Grassmarket since we were able to take the portal. Once we were there, the location of the scene was obvious. The streets were empty save for a massive crowd at the end of the neighborhood, near the entrance to The Vaults.

My stomach lodged in my throat as we approached, guilt rising like sludge inside me.

We were almost to the crowd when Ana appeared next to me, clearly having just arrived.

"I heard," she said. "This is awful."

"No kidding. Do you know when it happened?"

"They found the bodies a few hours ago."

That would coincide roughly with when the dark magic had burst out of me back in the jungle, destroying the guards. I shivered. If they killed again, maybe it would overtake me entirely. I remembered my worry that the explosions of dark magic within me led to the beasts feeding and prayed that wasn't the case. I couldn't help it when the magic exploded.

Oh fates, please don't let that be happening. I couldn't bear it if I were the cause of this.

We pushed our way through the crowd, Lachlan and Maximus using their bulk to move aside the crowd of looky-loos.

As before, the two bodies were sprawled in an alley. Their insides were now their outsides, what was left of them. Grief welled within me. These people had been innocent. And the monsters had devoured them, taking bits and pieces and leaving the rest.

On the far side of the alley, the Menacing Menagerie sat on a dumpster. Them again?

I left Maximus and Ana standing at the edge of the scene and hurried around the crowd, slipping in beside them.

"Funny finding you here. I'm starting to think this is more than a coincidence."

We like the adventure of finding our own trash. But this time, we found them, too. Romeo frowned. *This kind of stuff always happens in the darkness of alleys.*

Poppy and Eloise snuffled, as if agreeing with him.

The raccoon made a compelling point, which was something I'd never expected to think. "Did you find any other clues?"

There are more feathers. He pointed to them. *Lots and lots.*

Enough that there could be more than one monster. I shivered at the thought and hurried forward, nodding at the Protectorate guards who blocked the scene. They let me slip past.

Maximus was already in the middle, crouching down and inspecting a feather. Ana crouched near another, frowning. I joined her, peering down at it. Then I looked up and spotted Jude.

She crouched next to me. "Try your psychometros potion on it."

"Okay." A little thrill of excitement flowed through me at being asked to use my potion. It was a contribution only I could make, and it felt good, especially after being helpless for so long.

I picked up the feather and dug the little vial out of my belt, then dropped the tiniest drop onto it. The silver liquid soaked in, and I pressed my tongue to it.

"Ew," Ana muttered.

I agreed with her, but the words were stolen from my lips as a vision flashed in front of my mind. I gasped. "A mountain in the sea. There's a tiny, desecrated church on top. Feathers everywhere. It's their hideout."

I lowered the feather and looked at Ana.

"How did you see that this time?"

"Perhaps it was their most recent location. That's what led me to El Dorado. This feather was recently there, definitely."

Ana held out her hand, and I placed the feather in it. Her magic flared briefly, and she closed her eyes. "Yes, maybe I can track this with my Druid sense." She opened her eyes. "I'll get right on it."

"I'll go to Connor," I said. "If you can find the beasts, we'll find the counterspell. Then we'll go deploy it."

I glanced up to see Jude looking at us, and she nodded.

I stood, then searched for Maximus. He rose from where he was crouched by the bodies and came over to me, his face drawn. "Ready?"

"Ready."

We strode away from the crime scene, headed back toward the alley. I looked at Maximus. "The quickest way to Magic's Bend will be to take the portal back to the enchanted grove at the Protectorate. There's another portal in the woods that goes directly there."

It didn't take us long to take the two portals, though my head was spinning by the time I stepped out into the alley in the historic district in Magic's Bend. It was still light in Oregon, and the party was just getting started in this part of town. Most of the good bars and restaurants could be found in the historic district, and, as usual, this alley smelled vaguely like a urinal from last night's revelers.

I wrinkled my nose and stepped out onto the main street, sucking in a breath of fresh air, then hailed the first cab that passed.

The green-haired fairy behind the wheel turned around, popping her gum. "Where you headed?"

"Potions & Pastilles, on Factory Row," I said as Maximus slid in next to me.

"Got it." The fairy turned around and revved the engine, pulling away from the curb and flashing by old buildings painted in a rainbow of colors.

As one of the few all-magic cities in the world, Magic's Bend was a place where supernaturals could let it all hang out. Literally. A man with a long serpent's tail walked by on the street, and a trio of fairies fluttered their glittery wings as they walked, giggling and pointing at a shop full of scandalous dresses.

The cab passed quickly through the business district, flying by towering metal skyscrapers, then entered an older part of town. Factory Row had been revitalized about a decade ago, and Connor's shop was located in one of the buildings on the bottom floor.

The cabbie pulled over to the curb. "We're here."

"Thanks." Maximus handed her cash and climbed out.

I followed, pointing to the bar and coffee shop that had Potions & Pastilles scrolled across the window in gold. Light gleamed in welcome from behind the glass, but the place was mostly empty since it was midafternoon. After the coffee rush and before the cocktail and beer rush.

"I thought we were going to a potions master?" Maximus asked.

"We are. Connor runs this shop with his sister, Claire. But on the side, he's a potions expert and she's a mercenary."

"Sounds like this is a front for laundering money, then."

"You know a lot for a guy recently out of AD 99."

He just grinned and pushed open the front door.

I entered and sucked in the welcoming scent of coffee and Cornish pasties, the two afternoon specialties in the shop. In the evening, it would turn into a hipster whiskey bar.

Claire, Connor's dark-haired sister, was manning the bar this afternoon. She looked up from where she was wiping off the counter and grinned. "Rowan, long time no see. How are you?"

Her British accent was light after years of being in the States, but it was still there.

"Hey, Claire. Good, all in all." Okay, that was a bit of a lie, but now *was* the time for small talk. She'd help me in a flash if she knew I needed it, but I didn't want her to know I needed it. "We're here to see Connor about a potion."

She grinned and eyed Maximus, though she didn't ask who he was. "I'll go get him. Help yourself to anything in the pastry case."

As she ducked back into the kitchen to find Connor, I looked down into the glass case. It was full of savory pastries stuffed with meat and cheese and veggies—or some variation of that, since there were a lot of them. Claire and Connor had brought the recipes over from Cornwall when they'd moved years ago, and they were fantastic. I wasn't hungry after the sandwich, but I could probably use a coffee with a boost. We hadn't had any real rest in ages, and I was definitely dragging.

Maximus stood next to me, silently surveying the space. I

wanted to ask what he thought of it, but honestly, I didn't need to. He probably liked it. Who wouldn't? The coffee shop was done in warm wood with art on the walls and mason-jar lanterns hanging from the ceiling. It was very hipster trendy, but also welcoming.

The kitchen door swung open, and Connor walked out. He was only a couple years older than me, but slight and pale, with a flop of dark hair over his forehead. As usual, he wore a band T-shirt. Today it was Amy MacDonald; tomorrow, who knew?

He grinned. "I hear you have a potions question."

"We do. It's a doozy."

"Might as well come back." He gestured for us to come behind the counter.

Claire slipped out of the kitchen and into the bar. "Let me bring you a drink on the house. What'll it be?"

"A triple boosted latte, please," I said. They did the best magically enhanced coffees I'd ever had.

"Uh-oh." Her brows rose. "Long night ahead?"

"And behind." I couldn't quite remember the last good sleep I'd had.

"And for you, big guy?" Claire asked Maximus, eyeing him up and down. I didn't blame her. He did look pretty good. Scary, with all the muscles and the fighter's stance, but good. Heck, that was probably *why* he looked good.

"The same, thanks."

We followed Connor through the narrow kitchen and into his small workshop at the back. Every surface was cluttered with ingredients and glass vials and crucibles and tiny metal tools.

He turned to look at us. "What have you got?"

I handed over the two pieces of paper and the collection of little vials. "We're looking for a counterspell to a potion that allowed an ancient evil to rise again and feed on the living. The potion also makes the monster stronger. There's supposed to be a counterspell that will prevent the beast from feeding with its beak or claws, but Hedy couldn't make it. She thinks she didn't have the ingredients."

He paled a bit. "Feeding with its beak or claws? And it's feeding on people?"

"On people. The potion makes it strong, too. Without the counterspell, we don't have a chance of defeating it." I had a feeling that even *with* the counterspell, it'd be hard.

He nodded. "All right, then. Sounds like a priority."

"That's one word for it," Maximus said.

Connor gestured to two chairs squished up against the side wall. "You can wait there. This might take a moment."

"I'd like to watch, if that's all right."

"Sure." He began to fiddle with the various beakers and vials, his pale hands moving quickly. As he worked, he explained how he was analyzing the potion to try to figure out which ingredients would neutralize it. He tested several different things, a few of which smoked and bubbled. One sparked pink and another green.

At one point, Claire came in with our coffees. I sipped, delighting in the warmth and slight jolt of energy before I inevitably sagged again. We'd been through so much, and a coffee could only mask the effects of exhaustion this deep.

All the same, I watched Connor with avid interest. I hadn't always been into potions, but now that they were my biggest contribution to the magical world—what with my lame, funky magic—I realized that they were actually really interesting.

After about an hour, he finally turned, his eyes bright. "I think I've figured it out."

"Really?" I grinned. "You can make the counterspell?"

"I can, as long as you can get me the missing ingredient. Hedy was right. This one is difficult, and the ingredients are exceedingly rare." Connor's face turned grim. "Honestly, it's probably the reason that this potion was chosen. It's almost impossible to make the counterspell."

Maximus rose. "Where can we get the ingredient?"

"Unfortunately, it no longer grows in the wild. It's a rare flower called the *Mungeris Mitzeria*. It is red with yellow tips and a green center. Only one research lab has a sample of it. They grow it in their greenhouse."

"Where's the lab?" I asked.

He grimaced. "It's in the Swiss Alps. It won't be easy. Difficult to find, even harder to get into. And *out of*." He held up his hands when it was clear I was going to say we didn't have a choice. We *had* to get in, even if it meant risking it all. "I know, I know. You have to do it. Just be careful."

"It's in the middle of the mountains?" Maximus asked.

"It is, in an all-magical city called Interhorn. The whole place is owned by the research lab, though most people don't know that. They keep a low profile."

Maximus stood. "Can you show us on a map so that we can use a transport charm?"

"I wish I could. But they control entry to the city. It's partially a vacation destination, so that makes it a bit stupid, but the only way in is via train from Geneva. I think they keep such tight control because they're worried about theft from their lab, but I don't know that for sure."

I glanced at Maximus. "Then we'd better get a move on."

Connor pulled out his phone and fiddled with it, then looked up, his eyes bright. "You better hurry. The last night train into Interhorn leaves in an hour. Catch it at the train station on the edge of town in Geneva, in the supernatural district."

"Thanks." I gave him a quick hug, then turned and followed Maximus out of the shop. As I walked, I touched my fingertips to my comms charm and spoke briefly to Bree, asking her to let Jude know where we were going.

As soon as we were on the street, Maximus looked at me. "Ready?"

I nodded. Everything was easier in an all supernatural town. You could use a transport charm and disappear into thin air without worrying about humans seeing you.

He dug into his pocket and hurled a transport stone on the ground. Glittery silver dust exploded upward, and I stepped forward, letting the ether suck me in.

12

THE ETHER DRAGGED ME THROUGH SPACE AND SPIT ME OUT IN THE cold chill of Switzerland in the late winter. Immediately, I started shivering. Scotland was cold in the winter. So was Oregon. But definitely not Switzerland cold.

My gaze fell on one of the brightly lit shops that was on the bottom floor of an ornate old building. Winter parkas gleamed in the light.

"We're close to the train, right?" I asked.

"I think so."

I pointed toward the shop. "Let's make a pit stop, then, because it's freaking freezing."

"I'll conjure you one."

"Thanks."

His magic swelled, and he created me a warm puffy coat and pair of gloves. "Do you want a hat?"

"Not now, thanks." I took the coat and gloves. "Thanks. Don't you need one?"

"No. My demigod powers make me impervious to a lot."

I supposed if he was impervious to sword blows, then the cold definitely shouldn't bother him. I shrugged into the coat and inspected our surroundings. Street lamps sent a golden glow over the road, and the buildings had a distinctly romantic air to them, with ornate woodwork and glowing windows.

We hurried toward the train depot, dodging around human tourists and slipping into the all-supernatural district of town. It was hidden from human eyes by a glamour, but it wasn't hard for us to spot the glowing blue entrance through an alley.

I stepped out into the magical part of the city, immediately spying two vampires and a couple demons.

The demons were bold to be walking around in the open—they weren't even supposed to be on earth—but they weren't my problem right then. We had bigger fish to fry.

Across the street, the sign for the train depot stood tall over the entrance. We hurried over and bought two tickets in a sleeper car.

"I'd be lying if I said I wasn't excited about a few hours of sleep," I said.

Maximus nodded. "I wouldn't hate it myself."

The train billowed steam as we approached, and I wondered about the old-fashioned nature. But then, it was a tourist train, so maybe that was part of the appeal.

Then it began to move, slowly pulling away from the station.

Crap!

"Come on!" I sprinted forward, running for one of the sets of stairs that led onto the train.

A porter waved us forward, his jaunty blue cap perched on his head. "Hurry! No stopping now!"

I raced faster, running alongside the train until I reached the handrail and steps. I grabbed on and swung myself up, leaping onto the stairs and racing up to leave space for Maximus.

The porter grinned, a young kid with bright eyes. "That was close."

"Sure was." I glanced back.

Maximus swung up onto the car, not looking the least bit winded.

The porter directed us to our private car, leading the way through the antique hallways lit with gas lamps. It was like stepping back in time.

I grinned as we stepped into the train car, spotting the big window with a wide view of the passing city and the two bunk beds.

"We'll arrive in six hours." The porter handed us some papers. "Please sign these."

I took a clipboard with a sheet of paper on it. "What is it?"

"A waiver. If you experience grievous bodily injury or death on this trip, you will not sue us."

"What?" My jaw almost dropped. It had been so sweet and charming up until now.

"Bit of a dangerous journey, I'm afraid. No guarantee it'll be difficult, but we could encounter some trouble."

"Of what variety?" Maximus asked.

"Avalanche, monsters, demons wanting to waylay the train and rob us. The usual."

"For you, maybe." I scrawled my name on the page and handed it over.

Maximus did the same, and the porter left. I shucked off my jacket and my boots and gave Maximus a look, remembering our near-kiss from earlier. We were in a room with a bed. Two beds, which made it a bit better, but it still felt...intense.

"I'll take the top." The words contained only the slightest croak, and I was quite proud really. My blush, however...

That was one for the record books.

Fortunately, he said nothing and only nodded.

Was he thinking of it, too? I swore my skin was pulled so tight from the tension that I might burst. I did my best to ignore it and climbed onto the top bunk. Though my mind raced with the knowledge that Maximus was right below me, my body knew just what to do when it hit the softness of the bed. The rumble of the train lulled me, and I passed out in moments.

When the shouts came, I was having a delightful dream. One moment I was lounging on a beach, and the next, I was bolt upright in bed as someone shrieked, "Abominable Snowman!"

I leaned over the bed to look at Maximus, who sat upright also. "Abominable Snowman?"

"It can't be." He climbed out of bed and put on his boots.

I jumped down and followed his motion, zipping up my new warm jacket and grabbing my gloves. I threw my bag of potion bombs over my shoulder and headed out into the hall with Maximus. Most people stood in the open doorways of the compartments, though a few staff were running toward the back. We followed. The bar car was full of people with half-empty glasses and frightened eyes. The bartender had picked up a massive metal weapon.

"Is that a flame thrower?" I asked as we hurried past.

He nodded, gaze grim.

Maybe it really was the Abominable Snowman.

A roar rocked the car as we passed through, coming from the outside. I picked up the pace, wanting to see the monster. We hurried through a darkened car, and I looked out the window. Moonlight shined on massive mountains as the train zoomed through a steep valley. I'd bet a crate of double chocolate cookies that the tracks were perched on some kind of precarious bridge.

We made it out onto the back deck of the caboose just as the monster roared again. My eardrums rattled. I blinked in the darkness, my vision adjusting enough to take in half a dozen guards standing on the deck of the caboose, throwing fireballs at an icy monster that lumbered after us.

"It's an ice giant," Maximus said.

"Ice giant, Abominable Snowman. Six of one, half a dozen of another, really," I said.

He nodded.

The ice giant was at least one hundred feet tall, and agile as it raced along behind us, leaping over little valleys and massive boulders. The train was speeding along on top of a wooden bridge that was fifty feet tall. The monster towered above, reaching out with its hands to swipe at the caboose. He missed by about twenty feet, but he was gaining on us.

My heart thundered as I envisioned him making contact with the train.

"More fire!" shouted the commander of the guards. "It'll smash us to bits if it reaches us."

"It's just not slowing down!" shouted one of the mages.

All six of them hurled massive fireballs that lit up the night with an orange glow, but they only exploded off the monster's side, not doing much damage.

"It's the big beast," shouted the leader. "Unstoppable."

One of the mages next to me cursed. "The only time I sign up for this job and it's the big one that wakes."

"Does this happen often?" I asked, icy wind whipping against my face.

"No. Something is always waking in these mountains to chase the train. But this guy? He's rare."

The mages threw another round of fireballs at the ice giant, whose blue eyes gleamed in the light. He had massive fangs made of ice, and no doubt he saw this train as a moving snack car. He just had to smash us off the tracks, then pick up the people as they ran away. If they could run, after a fall like that.

I looked at Maximus. "We need to help."

He nodded, then shouted to the leader. "Does it have a weak spot? Your fire isn't working."

"It does, but it's on the head!" The leader looked at him with wild eyes. "The very top! No one can reach it, so we'll try to drive him off with our firebombs."

"They're *really* not working," I said.

"You want to try?" he demanded, his tone of voice making it clear that he thought I *wouldn't* accept his challenge.

"Heck yeah! Where's the weak spot *exactly*?"

"Right on top of the skull, in the middle, but good luck, lady."

I grinned at him. "Thanks."

"How do you want to do this?" Maximus asked.

"I've got a powerful stunning potion I can slam onto his head. As soon as he reaches out close enough, I'll jump on his arm and climb him." Even to my own ears, it sounded insane.

Maximus just grinned. "I like how you think. Race you to his head?"

I nodded. "What do I get if I win?"

He looked thoughtful.

Before he could respond, the leader shouted, "Incoming!"

I spun to face the back of the train. The ice giant was only about thirty feet away and gaining. He raised his arm to swipe at the caboose.

I turned to the leader. "If we stop him, you have to slow the train so we can catch up. No leaving us behind."

"If you stop him, I'll make you Queen of Switzerland."

"I don't think that's in your power, but I'll be happy if you stop the train."

He nodded sharply.

Maximus looked at me. "Ready?"

"Now or never." I tightened my bag of potions so it stuck to my back, then pulled on my new gloves and opened the back railing of the caboose, giving myself a platform to run and jump from.

The giant swiped out with his hand, and I raced for the edge of the caboose, then leapt off and grabbed onto his wrist. Fortunately, the giant was made of very craggy bits of ice. It gave me some good handholds to grip.

I clung to his forearm, stealing a quick glance below to see Maximus racing along the tracks and jumping onto the giant's hip. The train sped away as the giant roared and flailed, clearly realizing he had two stowaways. We probably felt like rats to him.

I clung tightly and began to scramble up his arm, grabbing tightly to knobs of ice. He flailed, trying to shake me off, but I held tight. If I fell, I was dead. All around, mountains loomed tall in the moonlight.

My heart lodged in my throat as his other hand slammed down on his arm, almost squishing me. I scooted around to the back of his bicep, then scaled higher.

When I made it to his shoulder, adrenaline was pumping so hard through my veins I thought I might be able to fly.

Honestly, this was probably the dumbest thing I'd ever done, but damned if it wasn't fun.

Below me, Maximus was almost to the shoulder. His eyes burned with intensity as he scaled the ice giant, who was now stomping around and shaking, trying to break us loose.

As fast as I could, I climbed up his neck and onto his head. The weak point in his skull was obvious. While the rest of his body was covered with a thick coating of ice, the top of his head looked like snow.

I yanked my potion bag around to my front and shoved my hand inside, searching for the round blue potion bomb that contained my most powerful stunner. The Murder Bomb. My hand gripped it, and I raised it high, then slammed it down on his skull, careful to withdraw my hand right before it smashed. I didn't want to get any of the liquid on me.

Maximus appeared at my side just as the liquid started

soaking into the giant's skull. The beast roared, flailing, then began to fall. He jerked sharply as he crumpled.

I lost my grip, slipping off the giant's head. A scream burst from my throat as my body met open air.

A strong hand gripped my wrist, yanking me to a stop.

Maximus.

I scrambled for a handhold, clinging to the giant's neck. I panted, holding on tightly.

But he was falling fast, and my safe position was going to last about a fraction of a second more.

"We have to jump!" Maximus shouted.

I searched frantically for the tracks, hoping to jump onto them, but we were too far away. The giant smashed onto the ground and began to roll.

Crap!

I leapt off his neck before he rolled over and crushed me, then scrambled upright in the snow. About twenty feet away, Maximus rose, his body covered in white.

The giant began to tumble down the mountainside, shoving piles of snow in front of him.

"There!" I pointed toward the tracks, which were about a hundred yards away.

The train was still moving.

"Hey! You jerks!" I waved my arms.

"They might think we're dead," Maximus shouted. His magic swelled on the air, the scent of cedar crisp against the snowy air. A flare gun appeared in his hand, and he pulled the trigger, firing the glowing light into the sky.

The train's brakes screeched, and the thing slowed.

"Thank fates for your conjuring." I trudged as fast as I could toward the train tracks, the deep snow coming up to my thighs.

Every muscle in my legs burned as I went. Maximus clearly went slower to allow me to keep up with him, and I wasn't going to complain. Last thing I wanted was to be left out here with the Snowman who would wake up eventually.

We reached the tracks and began to climb the wooden trusses that supported them. I climbed hand over hand, and was panting by the time I reached the top of the tracks, every muscle trembling. Maximus, who'd gotten to the top first, reached down and helped pull me up.

I flopped onto my belly, but gave myself only a moment. The train was stopped on the tracks in front of us, but it wouldn't wait forever.

"Come on." Maximus pulled me up.

Snow whipped against my face as I jogged along the tracks. "What do I win?"

"What do you mean?" His voice sounded suspiciously innocent.

"Don't play dumb. We were about to make a bet when we had to go after the Snowman. What would I have won if we'd finished? I did reach his head first, after all."

He frowned. "I don't know. What do you want?"

"A lot of things." Most of which he couldn't give me, in fact. I wanted my magic back. To pass the Academy. To get rid of the darkness inside me.

Pretty much the only thing I wanted from him that he *could* give me was a kiss. And that wasn't something I would say out loud.

"Let me think about it." I reached the back of the caboose and climbed on.

The six fire mages stared at us.

"Not bad," the leader said. His dark hair blew in the snowy wind, and he gave us an appraising look. "You sure you're just tourists heading to Interhorn?"

"Yep." I grinned and flexed my right arm. "I work out."

He gave me a skeptical look, but I slipped by him and

headed toward the main part of the train. The clock showed that it was nearly eight a.m., so we'd arrive pretty soon. At least I'd gotten plenty of sleep.

Maximus and I made our way toward the dining car and found an empty table. It didn't take long to order a breakfast of eggs and toast, and we ate fast.

When I finished, I looked up. "So, what's our story when we go through the border? The guard seemed to think we were tourists. We could go with that."

He nodded. "On vacation for a weekend." He frowned. "Is it the weekend?"

"I think it's Thursday."

"Early weekend. Then we'll slip through and find the research lab."

"I like this plan. Should be easy." As soon as the words left my mouth, I knew it'd been a dumb thing to say. Things that should be easy never turned out that way.

13

I HADN'T BEEN WRONG. PASSING THROUGH THE BORDER WASN'T easy. The lines were horrendously long through the cutesy little station. Decorative wood carvings were everywhere, along with gleaming fairy lights and the scent of hot chocolate.

But beneath it all, the scent of bureaucracy filled the air. The guards were highly regimented and the lines kept in meticulous order.

"Something is definitely fishy if a vacation destination is so closely guarded. This research lab is up to something," I whispered, eyeing a uniformed official in the distance who eyed me right back. I was squished in between some tourists from Canada and some others from Japan. They were supernaturals of some sort, but I couldn't tell what.

"By positioning themselves in a town like this, their staff has access to basic services," Maximus said. "And they can attract the best."

"Good point." It was a pretty place. I wouldn't mind working here. In fact, they probably were looking for good potion masters. Not that this was the life I wanted, but if the Protectorate kicked me out for having dark magic and being evil, then

I could come work here. I had a feeling they wouldn't mind if you were a little evil.

By the time I got up to the kiosk where a stony-eyed guard stared at us, I was grinning like a newlywed in love. Or at least, that was what I hoped it looked like. I clung to Maximus's side, enjoying the muscles of his arms, if I was being honest.

"Reason for your visit?" the guard grumbled. His magic was strong—three signatures. The scent of beeswax, the feel of cotton wool, and the taste of bread.

"Honeymoon." I gave Maximus googly eyes.

The guard frowned at us. "Then where are your rings?"

I scoffed at him. "We don't hold with such nonsense. Our love isn't on a physical plane, and it's definitely not so old-fashioned. We don't need that crap."

I actually wouldn't mind a ring if I ever got hitched, but we didn't have them, so my excuse was going to have to work. The guard gave Maximus a look like he was too cheap to buy me a ring. "Where are you staying in town?"

"The Swisslandic," Maximus said.

We'd heard another couple talking about it in the booth next to us at breakfast.

"What are your names?"

"He's Arthur Allbright, and I'm Katie McCorey. I didn't take his name." I figured it fit with our no-rings personas.

"All right." The guard began tapping into his computer, then frowned. "I see no Allbrights or McCoreys here. Everyone books before they come."

"We did." My heart started to pound a little bit harder. Crap, I hadn't realized that. There was no reason Connor should have known it either.

"They must have lost our reservation." Maximus sounded annoyed. I even bought it, though I knew this was all one big ruse.

The guard eyed us with renewed suspicion. Then he stood. "Come with me."

Holy fates, these folks didn't mess around. I looked at Maximus, who nodded.

The guard gestured to a man standing against the back wall. He wore a similar uniform and quickly took his place at the booth.

We followed our guard away from the crowd. Actually, this was better. If we couldn't easily sneak through the border, privacy was necessary.

The hallway that he took us to was much starker than the fairytale setting we'd left behind. Linoleum gleamed under fluorescent lights, and signs in German and French seemed to discuss safety, which was a bit weird for a supernatural town. A lot of the bureaucracy that plagued human cities didn't reach our kind. But this place was clearly run like a machine.

The guard led us back to a small room with a window up high. There were iron bars over it, but they weren't a problem. The main thing was that the window was big enough for us to shimmy out of.

We were alone, probably for an interview, though I doubted we'd be alone for long. I dug into the pouch of potions that hung along my side.

"Hands out of the bag," the guard barked.

I grinned at him and pulled out the potion bomb. It was a freezing potion, thank fates. I didn't want to kill the guy. With perfect aim, I threw the bomb and hit him in the chest. The glass exploded against him, and the liquid soaked into his shirt.

But he didn't pass out.

"What the heck?" He should already be on the floor.

An ugly expression crossed the guard's face as he reached for a red button on his shirt. An alarm.

But Maximus was too fast. He lunged for the guard, grabbed

his hands, yanked them behind him, then wrapped his arm around the guard's neck. The guard thrashed for a moment, then his eyes fluttered shut.

Maximus lowered him to the ground. "Sleeper hold. He should be out for an hour at least."

"Good." I dug into the belt at my hip and withdrew a forgetfulness potion. Carefully, I withdrew the eyedropper from the little bottle and squirted a tiny drop into each of the guard's eyes. "He'll forget everything he's seen for the last two hours. Should buy us some time."

"As long as they don't have security cameras," Maximus said.

"I saw none." And I'd been careful to look. "Hopefully they'll just think he fell asleep on the job and won't have a reason to question him." I glanced at the window. "Though, when we break out of that, it will be a pretty big clue."

Maximus walked toward the iron bars and reached for them, then hissed and yanked his hand back. "Protection charm."

"I'll take care of it." I reached into my belt and withdrew another little vial.

"What *don't* you have in there?"

"I'm like a Girl Scout. Prepared for anything." I pulled a chair over to the window and climbed onto it, then removed the top to the little vial and spritzed it on the iron bars. "It's like perfume, but it'll break through very mild protective enchantments. Nothing like El Dorado, but this isn't strong, I don't think."

As I'd suspected, this one wasn't super powerful. They valued the border here, but they planned for there to be a guard with you at all times. The magic around the iron bars snapped, and the electric current dissipated.

I stepped off the chair and gestured to the bars. "Your turn."

Maximus stepped up and yanked the bars straight off the window. Then he raised the glass window and hauled himself out, disappearing gracefully onto the street below. It was high enough that my escape was a little less graceful, but when I plopped to the snowy ground outside, I was pleased with myself.

I dusted my hands off and inspected the alley. The first thing I saw was a big trash bin with the lid off. The garbage inside was rustling around, and I had the eeriest feeling. Slowly, I approached, lifting up an old sandwich wrapper.

Eloise stared up at me, blinking owlishly into the light. The little badger grinned toothily. Poppy's head poked up next to her. The flower that the possum wore behind her ear had been replaced with a sprig of mistletoe.

"Festive, Poppy."

She just blinked at me.

Romeo's head appeared next. *Long time no see.*

"Why do you keep showing up where I am?"

We're your helpers. Magically ordained. Every Dragon God has helpers.

I lowered my voice so Maximus couldn't hear. "But I haven't gotten those powers yet."

If I ever would. All I had was this dark magic, and that certainly wasn't from the gods. If they were going to grace me with some of their magic, it certainly didn't seem to be happening any time soon.

Well, you've got us. We've taken a break from trash hunting one hundred percent of the time and are here to help you.

I blinked at him, unsure of what to say. Then I realized that Maximus was watching the exchange. I looked at him. "Can you hear them?"

He shook his head.

"I swear I'm not crazy."

"Sure."

I heaved a sigh, about to retort back. But a shout sounded from inside the room we'd just escaped. My gaze flashed to Maximus.

He jerked his head toward the alley exit.

We'll cover your trail!

I gave Romeo a grateful nod, then sprinted after Maximus. As I turned the corner, I spared one last glance at the alley, just in time to see the Menacing Menagerie leap onto the guard who'd shimmied out of the window.

Points for us.

A few feet out onto the main sidewalk, Maximus and I slowed to a walk. It wouldn't do to look suspicious, and we still had a few moments before the guards made it out the front door of the border control and onto the main street.

The town itself was lovely, a perfect Swiss ski town with ornate wooden buildings, chimneys billowing smoke, and white mountains in the backdrop. Skiers walked around in snow gear, while shoppers were bundled up to their ears. It was a proper little city, right in the mountains.

"Nothing looks like a research lab," Maximus said.

"No, I don't suppose it would." I studied all the buildings that we passed, unable to see anything that stood out from the rest. They all had comparable magic signatures as well.

It only took us about an hour to scan every street and building in the city, but none of them were our target.

"I think the magic signature of the place must be blocked," Maximus said. "Even if it looks the same as the rest, we should be able to feel it."

He had a point. Whatever they were doing in the lab would give off some serious magic vibes, but I felt nothing.

"Hang on, I have something for that." I grinned as I dug into my belt.

I sprinkled a tiny bit of the potion on the back of my hand, and it began to tingle immediately.

Maximus frowned at my hand. "What does it do?"

"Enhances my ability to feel great magic." My hand tingled

especially strong when I put it near him, in fact. "Even concealed magic. Can you walk twenty feet behind me? You're screwing up my reading."

He nodded and stepped back, drifting away down the street. I held up my hand and spun in a circle. It prickled particularly strongly when facing east, so I headed down the street, following it.

Soon, I reached the edge of town, where a ski slope led upward. There weren't any skiers on it, though there were tracks leading down. A gondola moved upward, the cars swaying slightly in the wind.

I turned back to Maximus and gestured him forward, speaking only once he was close. "I think it's slightly outside of town. That way, maybe in the trees."

"I can see a bit of a chalet."

I squinted, and caught sight of the brown wooden building through the trees. The gondola was leading to it, in fact, though there was only one person riding it. "Let's walk."

He nodded. "Probably not a recreational ski slope, and we're not very good at faking it."

"No Oscars for us." I stepped off the city sidewalk and into the snow, realizing that my leather boots might keep the snow out, but my toes were going to be frozen by the time we reached the top.

I ignored the cold as we climbed, sticking to the shadow of the trees. No skiers zoomed past us, but my hand prickled more fiercely as we got closer. Once we reached the building, we hid in the trees, spying.

The chalet was a large structure, at least forty feet tall with a domed glass structure on part of the roof.

"It's an arboretum, where they grow things," I murmured.

"There are two guards at the gate. This place will go on lock-down if we try to force our way in."

"Lockdown? You sure know a lot of slang for someone born in another millennium."

"My brief time with a mercenary guild was a real crash course in this sort of thing. And I made a point to assimilate quickly."

He was a survivor, that was clear. And assimilation always helped with that.

I turned back to the building just in time to see two people step out of a side door. They strode toward a rack that was covered in skis, each of them wearing a pair of big plastic boots. "They're going to ski down."

"Done for the day, perhaps."

"They can always change their minds." I shifted through the trees, moving closer to them. "Come on. Help me grab them."

"You have a plan."

"A good one." And it'd give me a chance to use one potion I'd never gotten to try. Maybe I wasn't so helpless after all. Not if I had my liquid arsenal.

As quickly and quietly as I could, I raced toward the two scientists. At least, that was what I assumed they were. They wore glasses and looked very pale, so it wasn't the worst assumption. As long as they had name badges and access passes, they would work for our purposes.

Fortunately, they were putting on their skis near the tree line, around the corner of the building and out of sight of the guards at the front. I reached them at the same time Maximus did. I lunged for the smaller one and wrapped one arm around his throat while my other went around his mouth.

I tried the sleeper hold that I'd seen Maximus use, and it worked. The little guy sagged in my arms after a few seconds. "I hope I didn't kill him."

"You didn't. And you're a quick study." Maximus laid his unconscious scientist on the ground.

"Thanks." Quickly, I unbuckled the skis from my guy's feet, then looked around for a place to stash him. I couldn't just leave him in the snow, so it needed to be warm. There was a shed about a dozen yards away. "Let's try to put them there."

I started to drag my guy, but Maximus held up a hand. "I've got it. We don't want body tracks."

He threw one man over each shoulder, then started hoofing it toward the building. The shed was actually a small heated garage full of snowmobiles and gasoline containers. I eyed the machines with interest as I grabbed a few long rags off a table and used them to bind the hands and mouths of the men.

"It looks like they use this place often, so they should find them fairly soon." Which was good, actually. I didn't want them dying of starvation in here. I didn't know if they were evil baddies, so I didn't want to be responsible for their deaths. "Get their name badges and any identification or access cards."

We rifled through their pockets and found lanyards with identification. There were no keys or access cards, but then, magical places didn't often have those, so I didn't worry.

"We don't look like them, though." Maximus eyed my handy belt. "Unless you have a glamour potion in there."

"Indeed, I do." I pulled it out. "I've never used it, though, so there's no guarantee it will work. There's one gross part though." I grimaced as I bent and pulled a hair out of my guy's head. "It's really unfortunate."

Maximus frowned. "Really?"

I popped the hair in my mouth and took a tiny swig of potion. "Yep."

Chills raced down my skin as the potion made it to my stomach. Pain followed, a deep ache that made me wince.

Maximus studied me intently.

"Well?" I asked.

"Well, you make a decent-looking man."

I grinned, holding out my hands to inspect them. It had worked!

The scientist's hands weren't much bigger than mine, but they certainly were different. And my clothes had even changed. Fantastic.

Maximus repeated the drill, shrinking about eight inches and turning into a beady-eyed scientist with a full head of very messy blond hair and a pair of glasses.

"Let's go." I didn't know exactly how long this potion would last, so we really needed to get a move on.

We went toward the side door where the scientists had exited earlier, but there was no door handle and nowhere to show our ID card to maybe ignite some magic. Quickly, I inspected the edges of the door, but couldn't find a way to open it.

"We'll have to try the front," Maximus said.

I nodded and followed him around to the front entrance where the two guards were manning the front door.

"Thought your shift was over?" grumbled the larger one, who stood on the right.

"Left my notebook," I said.

The guard gave me a suspicious look, then turned his gaze to Maximus. I swallowed hard.

Would he buy our disguises? Was my glamour holding up?

14

Next to me, I could feel Maximus trying to look meek. It worked pretty well, but only because he was wearing the glamour. He'd never look meek in his normal size.

"Fine, but hurry," the guard snapped. "You shouldn't be in after your shift."

I nodded and slipped past, slipping through the door with Maximus on my heels. I had no idea what floor these guys normally worked on, but we needed to reach the top. Hopefully, the plant would be growing in the greenhouse.

"Place reeks," Maximus murmured.

I took a tentative sniff and got a whiff of all sorts of magic, both dark and light. Doors were closed all along the hallway, but each emitted a different signature. Signs in French and German were plastered to each door, but I had no idea what they said. The halls were made of the same dark wooden planks as outside, and the whole place had an air of Swiss chalet instead of research lab.

We strode confidently back toward a set of stairs at the end of the hall and began to climb. The first two flights went without incident, but the third had a metal gate in front of it.

I stood back and studied it, frowning. “Definitely some kind of protection charm. Nothing that my potions will work on.”

Maximus studied the wooden wall at the side of the gate, then slammed his fist against it.

I jumped and hissed, “What the heck!”

“Apparently your glamour doesn’t take away our powers.” He grinned and grabbed the wooden plank that now had a hole in it. He pulled it away, and then yanked off a few more. The movement seemed effortless. He kept going until he’d torn away enough of the wall that we could slip through at the side of the gate.

“Well, that’s one way to go about it,” I muttered as I squeezed around the gate, careful not to lose my footing and get wedged in the wall.

Once on the other side, we started climbing more stairs, moving as quickly as we could. The building was quiet, but eventually someone would find the destruction. They might not recognize us as the cause, but better safe than sorry.

We passed the third floor, but didn't stop to explore. Connor had said that the *Mungeris Mitzeria* would be in the greenhouse at the top.

When we reached the highest door, I stopped and stared at it. The wood was thick and dark, and I could definitely feel a protection charm.

I ran my hands around the edges of the door, trying to get a feel for the kind of charm that protected it.

"How strong is it?" Maximus asked.

“Fairly weak, but I think that’s because the protection charm is behind the door, not on the door itself.”

"Ready to open it, then?"

In response, I turned the doorknob and pushed it open. The door swung wide without issue, revealing a massive laboratory filled to the brim with vials of ingredients, glass beakers, equipment of all varieties, and dozens of potion books.

My eyes widened. I hadn't been born with an innate interest in potions, but I'd really become obsessed lately. I'd love to spend time wandering around here. But time was the last thing we had.

Right in front of us, a thick heavy purple mist rose up from the floor. I coughed, the smoke burning the back of my throat.

"What is it?" Maximus stepped back.

I stared hard at the smoke, frowning. I thought I'd seen something like this once, in one of Lachlan's potion books. But what had it said? Definitely that the smoke was poisonous. So far we were fine, but we couldn't breathe much more. I glanced around, looking for something to stop the smoke. Since there was no charm on the door, it meant that the smoke would rise up every time someone entered, even if they were an employee. So I had to find some kind of antidote, or something to make it stop.

There was a shelf to the left of my head, right next to the door. Hundreds of vials of potions sat on it, as if they were waiting for just this opportunity. I wouldn't be surprised if some were even placebos, meant to distract the unwitting and unwelcome visitor.

"I need to find something to counteract the smoke." I bent down and sniffed gingerly at the wafting poison, needing to get a better idea of what it was made of. I coughed violently, my throat burning.

"Be careful!" Maximus grabbed my arm and pulled me back.

"I know what I'm doing." Mostly.

I focused on the scent of the smoke, picking up the distinctive smell of lilacs. My mind raced, trying to remember what I'd read in the book. There was something to counteract it, a liquid that would diffuse it quickly.

Lilacs, lilacs, lilacs...

My memory clicked into place, and excitement flared in my chest.

I spun back to the shelves stuffed full of potions, searching them. I tried to breathe shallowly, not wanting to inhale too much of the smoke. "I'm looking for a murky brown potion the color of black mud. It's actually a liquid made of coal dust, and it should counteract the lilac smoke."

I grabbed several off the shelf and peered more closely at them. Maximus handed me a couple as well.

Only one of them looked like it was made of floating particles of coal dust suspended in clear liquid. I put the other four potions back, and turned to the smoke.

My lungs burned from holding my breath. I uncorked the glass vial and splashed the liquid onto the smoke. There was a brief hissing sound, then the smoke disappeared.

I gasped, gratefully sucking in air, as my heart pounded in my ears.

The stone floor beneath my feet was speckled with the dark potion, clearly showing hundreds of applications of the black liquid.

I looked at the glass vial in my hands and grinned when I saw what I expected. It was already refilling with the coal dust potion.

"Remind me what the flower looks like?" Maximus asked.

"It's red with yellow tips and green center. About the size of your palm."

Maximus pointed toward the glass ceiling where dozens of hanging baskets were hooked onto the rafters where they got the best sunlight from the glass roof above. Each was filled with flowers. Unfortunately, they were so high it was difficult to see inside the baskets.

I stepped deeper into the laboratory, keeping my eyes peeled for any scientists or guards who might already be there. If they were, they might not realize that we were intruders. We still looked like the scientists, and I hadn't hesitated long before pulling down the proper potion to diffuse the smoke that guarded the space.

“Hello?” I called, deciding to get it over with.

If someone were here, it was better to know about it now. I didn't want them seeing us and realizing that we weren’t supposed to be here, even if we did look like employees. The ones we were impersonating might not even work on this level, and I didn’t want some guards showing up because I hadn’t noticed this place was already occupied.

But there was silence all around us, and my shoulders relaxed. "I think we’re alone."

"Good, let's make this quick." Maximus climbed up onto a table next to me, his movements graceful and quick. "It's easier to see from up here.”

I mimicked his motions, climbing onto another table on the other side of the room and searching for any baskets that contained a red flower. There were many, but none that contained exactly the right one.

I pulled down a couple to get a better view, still unable to find what I was looking for.

"Is this it?" Maximus's voice sounded from across the room.

I turned, spotting the flower gripped in his hand. It looked almost right—the colors were all there. But they weren't exactly the right shade, and the shape was slightly off.

I shook my head. "No, I don't think so,"

I wished that Romeo, Eloise, and Poppy were here. They had such a great sense of smell that they could probably find this flower in no time.

I was digging through another hanging basket full of various blooms when a voice sounded behind me. "Hey! What are you doing in there? You shouldn't be on the tables."

Oh crap. I turned, reaching into the potion bag that I'd slung over my side. My hands unerringly found the sleeping potion that came in a triangular glass bomb.

The woman in front of me was pale, with blonde hair and blue eyes that were nearly translucent. She looked like she hadn't seen the sun in a decade. Her glasses were perched on her nose and her hair tied up in a messy bun. Probably scientist.

She stood there with her arms propped on her hips, and a glower on her face. "You know you're supposed to use the ladders. I don't care if it's faster to climb on the tables, it's not proper lab protocol."

Oh yeah, definitely a scientist.

I threw the potion bomb. Her pale eyes widened just briefly before the glass slammed into her chest. The liquid exploded over her, blue and gleaming. She didn't even have a chance to scream. Her eyes rolled back in her head, and her body sagged.

Maximus leapt to the floor and raced to her, grabbing her before she hit the ground. He laid her carefully under the table where she wouldn't get stepped on.

"She'll wake up in about an hour," I said.

"Good." He climbed onto the table again and resumed his search.

I kept hunting, and when I finally saw the flower, my heart jumped. I was about to reach for it when a voice sounded from the comms charm around my neck.

"Rowan!" It was Bree. "We found the beast's lair. How close are you to finding the missing ingredient? No one else has had any luck."

"Just found it." I grinned. "We just need to get back to the train depot so that we can transport out of here. This whole place is protected by a non-transport spell." I hadn't even finished my sentence when a siren blared through the room. "Oh crap, Bree. We've got to go. I think they figured out we're here."

"Hurry, and be safe!"

"You too." I plucked a dozen blooms and packed them in a tiny plastic box, then shoved them in my jeans' pocket. I jumped off the table and looked at Maximus. "Let's get the hell out of here."

He yanked the door open and hurried out onto the stairway. We raced down the stairs as fast as we could, joining other employees as they surged toward the exits. Whatever that alarm had been, no one wanted to stick around.

For a while it seemed like we might be able to just flow out with the crowd, blending in with them. But when we hit the main entry hall, two guards spotted us, scowls creasing their faces.

One pointed and shouted, "Hey you! Stop!"

Crap.

"Run," Maximus said.

I sprinted forward through the crowd, shoving one hand into my bag of potions. When I found the stunning potion, I yanked it free and hurled it at guards' feet. It slammed into the ground in front of them, the glass shattering and the smoke billowing up. The guards plowed right into it and immediately started choking. A moment later, they fell over.

I leapt over their bodies as we raced out of the building and across the snowy lot, heading for the skis that had been abandoned on the ground earlier.

Shouts sounded from behind, guards yelling at us to stop in English, French, and German. As if I'd suddenly hear *halt* and stop dead in my tracks.

Ha. No way in hell that was gonna happen.

Fortunately, the glamour potion not only made us look like

the scientists—we wore their clothes as well. I slammed my ski boots onto the skis, grateful to hear them click as they attached. I grabbed the ski poles that had fallen to the ground.

Maximus and I pushed our way toward the ski slope that would get us away from here.

To our left, eight guards sprinted toward us, each dressed in identical dark blue uniforms. Four of them pulled out magical stunners that looked like wands. I'd only ever seen them demonstrated at the Protectorate, but they could hurl a massive jolt of magic that would shock a person so hard, they'd wet their pants and pass out.

No way going to be me.

I picked up a little momentum with my ski poles, then reached into my potions bag and found the one that was the equivalent of a banana peel in a cartoon. I hurled it at the guards, then dug my ski poles into the snow, zipping forward. I turned back to look at the guards and spotted them piled on the ground, struggling to rise in the snow.

I reached the top of the hill, and my skis tipped over. I whizzed down the hill behind Maximus as wind burned my eyes, and I prayed I wouldn't fall.

Overhead, the roar of a helicopter broke through the quiet of the day. I looked up, catching sight of a guard hanging out the door, ready to hurl potion bombs at us.

Oh crap.

I turned right, zigzagging down the slope as the guard threw potion bombs down at us. They crashed into the snow, exploding with black smoke and splashes of red liquid.

"Almost there!" Maximus shouted from ahead.

I dug my ski poles harder into the snow, gaining speed. The helicopter swooped above, diving lower so the guard could get a good shot. He flew in front of me, so close that I could see the blue of his eyes.

I barely managed to avoid the bombs he hurled. Soon, I spotted a clump of tightly packed evergreen trees at the base of the hill. They'd provide a little cover, so I skied right for them, plowing into the evergreens as a potion bomb hit me in the shoulder, exploding against my jacket.

I fell into the snowy trees, branches scratching my face and neck. The trees provided a little cover as I tore off my jacket, my shoulder burning with pain.

Ahead of me, Maximus yanked off his skis and reached for me, pulling me through the trees.

"This way," he said. "There's a building."

The cluster of evergreens was pressed up against a small building, and we slipped inside. The space was no bigger than my apartment, full of various tools and cans of gasoline. Another work shed.

Maximus still looked like the nerdy scientist, and I was sure I did, too. I was still wearing his ski boots after all. I dug into my potion belt and yanked at the antidote, then took a little swig and passed it over to Maximus, pain already tearing through my muscles as I transformed.

He drank the rest, and within seconds, he looked like himself.

"Maybe they won't recognize us now, and we can sneak to the train station to transport out of here." I searched for a second exit—one that didn't lead into trees and a ski slope—and found it.

We exited into an alley, and I kept my gaze trained at the sky, searching for the helicopter. I could hear it but didn't see it.

When we made it out onto the main street in town, the atmosphere was tense. Tourists kept glancing up at the helicopter. I looked, too, pretending to be confused, but I walked as quickly as I could toward the station.

"Hey you!" a gruff voice shouted from behind us.

I didn't have to turn to know it was a guard.

"Run!" Maximus sprinted forward, and I followed, my heart thundering.

We raced past shops and restaurants, darting around people and jumping over benches. We were so close to the train station. We just had to get past the tracks, to the outskirts of the village where the transport blocking charm no longer worked.

Fortunately, there was no long line to get into the train station, probably because there was no train this time of day.

"Guards in front," I shouted, spying a few of them at the entrance to the station.

Maximus veered left to avoid the guards, and I followed.

"Hey!" Their shouts echoed through the street.

We sprinted by, not stopping, and spilled out onto the train platform. As I'd suspected, there was no train there.

"Get across the tracks!" Maximus shouted.

I leapt onto the tracks and ran across, my feet sinking into the soft snow on the other side. Next to me, Maximus reached into his coat pocket and pulled out a transport charm, then hurled it to the ground.

The glittery gray smoke burst up, and I lunged into it. At the last second, I glanced over my shoulder, spotting the angry faces of the guards as they jumped onto the track in pursuit.

15

MAXIMUS JUMPED INTO THE SMOKE RIGHT AS THE ETHER SUCKED me in and spun me through space. A moment later, it spat me out on the front lawn of the Protectorate.

I gasped, whirling around to see Maximus appear out of thin air behind me. No guards arrived behind him, thank fates.

Panting, I propped my hands on my knees. "Holy fates, that was close."

"Too close." Maximus was only slightly out of breath, but it was the most winded I'd ever seen him. "I've never skied before."

"You did well."

"You didn't see my dismount." He shot me a wry smile.

A laugh escaped me.

"Rowan! Maximus!" Jude's voice sounded from the castle. "Did you get the ingredient?"

I turned toward Jude, catching sight of her standing on the main steps, her starry blue eyes bright on us.

"We did!" I hurried toward her, then jumped up onto the castle steps as I dug into the pocket of my jeans and pulled out the little plastic box of flowers.

"Excellent."

Footsteps thundered down the stairs at the main entry, and I peered around to see Hedy, making way too much noise for someone so small.

"We've got it!" I held up the flowers.

"Excellent!" She raced toward me, grabbed the flowers out of my hands, and kept running, right onto the lawn and in the direction of her workshop. "I'll have it done in an hour. Two, tops!"

I turned to go after her, but Jude grabbed my arm. "She can show you how to make the potion later. Right now, there's a briefing in the round room for anyone going on the mission to confront the demons and their beast. I assume you want to be part of that?"

"I do!"

Jude looked at Maximus. "You, as well?"

He nodded sharply.

"Come on, then. Your sisters are waiting, Rowan."

We hurried up the stairs and down the hall, entering the round room to find the table pretty full. Ana and Bree sat there, along with their boyfriends, Cade and Lachlan. Caro, with her platinum blonde bob and thousand-watt smile sat next to the dark-haired twins, Ali and Haris.

Caro's silver eyes darted to me. "We heard you got the necessary ingredient?"

"We did."

She grinned widely. "Well done."

Ali and Haris nodded, leaning back in their chairs.

"This will be a good fight, then," Ali said.

Jude took a seat at the head of the table. Though it was round and there technically was no *head*, wherever Jude sat seemed to be imbued with extra importance.

I sat next to Bree, and Maximus sat next to me.

Ana leaned forward, her blonde hair swinging over her

shoulder. "Our scouting mission revealed that the demons have a headquarters on a tiny, unnamed island between Greece and Turkey."

"Unnamed?" Maximus frowned. "I thought every rock in that sea had a name."

"They do. *If* they're on a map," Bree said. "This island was on no map. In fact, clouds hid it for the first two hours of our visit. It took a while to find it, and we only saw it once we were in the sky."

"It's located closer to Turkey than to Greece," Ana said. "And it seems like it's only a temporary headquarters. There's not much on the island besides the demons and their beasts in a tiny, decrepit church."

My head jerked up at the plural. "Beasts, as in more than one?"

"We think they have two," Jude said.

"Crap." I frowned. I'd been worried about that. "Did I get enough flowers for the potion?"

"Hedy seemed pleased," Maximus said.

"Good point." I looked at everyone. "So, what's the plan, then?"

"According to Hedy, the birds need to drink the potion. Or at least, get some in their mouths. Their feathers repel other potions."

Fantastic. That would be *super* easy.

"We were thinking that Ana and I could attack from the sky," Bree said. "Draw the beasts out and deliver the potion. Cade, Lachlan, and Maximus could approach the island with the rest of the PITS. They'd go by boat. There, they would take out the demons and find their leader. Hopefully figure out their end goal."

"What about me?" I asked. I wanted a chance to grill some demons about this dark magic. Even if I did manage to dampen it by stopping the beasts from feeding, I needed to figure out what it was and how to get rid of it entirely.

"Your aim is the best," Jude said. "You can ride on Ana's back and throw the potion at the monsters. Get it in their mouths and we succeed."

"Seriously?" How the hell would I throw a potion into the beak of a giant bird beast? My mind raced with ideas.

"That's the tricky part," Jude said.

"No kidding." Not that I wanted to wrestle one of those giant monsters to get the potion into their mouths. Throwing seemed better. "But what do I say, 'open up'?"

A few people chuckled at my sing-song voice.

"We need a way to *force* them to open their mouths," Maximus said. "To compel them."

I chewed on my lip, thinking. "I do have a potion that makes you feel like you're suffocating. It won't kill them, but they might open their mouths to get more air."

Cade grinned, his brown hair gleaming. "I like how you think."

I smiled at him. I'd always liked Bree's boyfriend. He was a shifter and a Celtic god of war, and he was head over heels for Bree. They were a great match.

"That means we have a plan," Jude said. "Deploy the potions. Once the monsters are weakened, take them out. Don't get too close before they are bound, however. You won't stand a chance. The rest of the team will take out the demons and find their leader."

Easy peasy.

Well, maybe not. But I was looking forward to the challenge.

Three hours later, after some food and a quick change of

clothes, I found myself standing on the shore of western Turkey, staring at the sea. Night was beginning to fall, sending a golden pink glow across the rippling surface of the water. Fresh salt air blew my hair back from my face, and it felt more like the beginning of a vacation than the start of a battle.

The tension in the air drove that feeling away quickly, though.

Ali, Haris, and Maximus pushed the small boat toward the crashing surf. Cade, Lachlan, and Caro waited, ready to board.

I squinted across the ocean, toward a cluster of low-hanging clouds. If I squinted in just the right way, I thought I could make out the island they hid.

"Took us ages to find it," Ana said. "Could only see it from the air, in fact."

"Thank fates you did." Ana had the powers of The Morrigan, a Celtic battle and fate goddess who could also turn into a giant crow. I'd ride her into battle, something we'd only practiced a handful of times before.

The little boat splashed into the water, and Maximus looked at me. Though we were separated by at least twenty yards, I could see something heavy in his eyes. Something like worry.

For me?

No way.

I nodded at him and turned away. Ana and Bree kissed Cade and Lachlan quickly, then told them to be careful. The crowd of six piled into the little rowboat. Maximus took the oars, and it shot off across the water. If it didn't make any noise at all, the demons might not even notice their approach.

I turned to Ana and Bree. "Ready?"

"Born ready." Ana grinned and propped her hands on her hips, looking like a caricature of a superhero. She'd always been a goofball. "I'm off."

She turned and ran, sprinting into the distance. When she

was about twenty yards away, she shifted into the form of a massive black crow. Her huge wings carried her into the air, and she wheeled around on an air current and returned to me and Bree, landing gracefully at my side.

"Good luck, and be safe," Bree said. "Remember—three tries."

I patted the potion bag strapped to my back. I could do this. I *had* to do this. Hedy had only been able to make three potions, so I could afford just one mistake.

Bree drew her sword as her wings unfurled from her back, silver and bright. She leapt into the sky.

I turned to Ana and climbed onto her back, gripping her feathers tight. She cawed and took off. Wind tore at my hair as we rose and swept down over the ocean.

The little rowboat was nearly halfway across. Not bad. They'd be there in another five minutes, if they were lucky.

Something splashed to their left. I squinted.

Please be a mermaid. Or a friendly fish.

The splash came again, revealing a long worm-like creature. Fangs glinted in the light of the setting sun.

Damn.

There were more splashes all around, closing in on the boat. Could they see that the monsters were coming?

"Ana, look down there!"

Ana's big black head tilted to the side so she could see down, then she dived. She hurtled toward one of the sea monsters, then scooped the thing up in her beak and chomped it in half. The two pieces of the giant serpent fell.

I dug into my potions bag and withdrew a bomb that could freeze a creature that size. I sucked in a deep breath and threw. It exploded against the creature's head, and it hissed and went down.

There were still a half dozen, and the people in the boat hadn't noticed. They were too low to the waterline.

As if she'd read my mind, Ana dipped down. She carried me right over the top of the boat, so close that I could say, "Sea serpents coming!"

Ana flew high up into the sky, whirling around again to re-approach the boat and the serpents.

Bree had flown low over the sea to attack with a sword, and Ali and Haris jumped into the ocean. Two sea serpents darted for them, cutting through the water. My heart leapt into my throat even though I'd already seen the two djinns pull their possession trick.

As the serpents neared, Ali and Haris's golden skin turned transparent, and they drifted into the sea monsters, becoming one with them. Suddenly, the sea monsters turned their attack toward their fellows, commanded by Ali and Haris. The djinns possessed them, commanding them to fight the other serpents.

The fight was over within minutes, bringing only the sound of splashing.

"Thank fates," I muttered. "Let's get the real fight started."

We flew toward the island, and the boat beached on the rocky shore. The tall mountain rose up behind it, and up this close, I could see a building on the top. It looked like a very old church, the top decorated with a cross.

Ana flew over to Bree, whose silver wings kept her hovering in one place.

"Ready?" I asked.

They both nodded.

Ana began to screech, a loud crow's call that made my hair stand on end. Movement in the church caught my eye, and demons spilled out. They raced toward a set of narrow stone stairs that led down to the beach where our colleagues waited to fight.

Two massive bird-like creatures burst out of the church. In the light of the setting sun, I could see them better than I ever had before. They did look a bit like owls, though the figure of a woman flickered over them occasionally. Then the image of a horrible fanged monster.

Their magical signature was so powerful, it almost bowled me over.

"Now or never." I dug my hand into my pouch and grabbed my square potion bomb full of the poison that would make them feel like they couldn't breathe.

"Over here!" Bree shouted, waving her sword. "You're so ugly even a dog wouldn't kiss you!"

Despite the fear that chilled my skin, the smallest laugh escaped me. I doubted the bird beasts understood English, but one of them charged Bree, who would hold it off until I could get to it. The other charged Ana, its powerful wings carrying it toward us.

Ana shot upward, and I leaned over her side. My heartbeat roared in my ears as I watched the beast chase us, gleaming black eyes glued to us. I raised the potion, ready to throw.

But the beast was fast, nearly to us.

I hurled the potion bomb through the air and nailed the creature right on the beak where it had two little nostrils. The glass exploded, and the potion burst out in a cloud of blue smoke. The monster sucked it in.

In the distance, Bree fought with the other creature, swiping out with her sword and going for the throat.

The potion took a moment to work, so I drew my sword from the ether and lunged out, aiming for the bird's neck.

The creature dodged, barely avoiding my blade but swiping out with a claw. It dragged across my shin and Ana's feathered side, and we both cried out in pain.

Then the beast's beak opened as it gasped for air.

"The potion is working!" I dug into my bag and found one of the three round potion bombs that Hedy had made. "Go higher!"

Ana swooped upward. My shin burned with pain and droplets of blood fell, but I ignored it and focused on the bird below. It flapped its wings frantically as it tried to breathe. From experience, I knew that it could get a little air in—this wouldn't kill it—but it was definitely weaker and struggling for air.

"Left!" I shouted.

Ana dodged left, trying to get into a position from which I could throw. I caught sight of the battle on the beach where Maximus fought with the PITs and Cade and Lachlan. There were at least two dozen demons, and magic flew left and right, the fighting fierce.

I turned my attention back to the bird. Its beak gaped open. This was it.

As carefully as I could, I aimed. The wind tore at my hair as Ana flew toward the struggling beast. I threw my potion bomb, watching as it soared through the air and exploded into the mouth of the bird.

The creature shrieked, suddenly able to breathe again. The first potion had worn off, and the creature was enraged. It hurtled toward us, so fast that we couldn't escape. I prayed the potion had worked.

The monster shifted in midair so it could claw us with its talons. But when it was only two feet way, it stopped abruptly.

A shriek of rage unlike any I'd ever heard filled the night.

The beast was bound!

It flew away, shaking its feet and trying to figure out what was wrong. It was no longer a threat to us, though.

"To the other beast!" I shouted.

Ana didn't need to be told twice. She whirled on the air and flew toward Bree and the other monster. Blood dripped down

Bree's cheek from a cut and her eyes were wild, but she was holding it off. Damn, the monster was strong, if it could get a swipe in on Bree.

"Fly over them!" I shouted to Ana.

The other beast was so distracted by Bree that it didn't notice us flying overhead. I grabbed one of the strangling potion bombs from my bag and hurled it at the monster bird's beak. It smashed into it, the plume of blue smoke rising high, and the creature sucked in the smoke.

Bree darted away, knowing enough to hold her breath.

It didn't take long for the second monster to open its mouth. I hurled the potion bomb at the bird's mouth, victory surging through me.

Right before it made contact, the monster closed its beak. The glass shattered against it.

Shit!

I only had one bomb left. The spare.

My mind raced. Did I risk it?

No.

"Fly right over the monster!" I shouted.

Ana squawked, clearly knowing what I wanted to do. If she were able to speak English in this form, she'd be saying "Hell no, it's too dangerous!"

"I can do this!"

She squawked again, but finally relented, diving low. I spared the fighters on the beach one last glance and saw that the battle was still going strong.

Then we were over the beast, and I leapt onto its back, the wind tearing at my hair as I fell. The creature shrieked and thrashed. I clung for dear life, desperate not to lose my grip. Wind made my eyes water, but I managed to shimmy up the bird's back and get closer to its beak.

One of the bird's talons somehow managed to swipe my

thigh, and pain bloomed. I clung tighter to the bird, ignoring the searing agony. It clawed again, delivering another blow.

Damn, this thing was fast.

With every second that passed, it felt like my heart thundered louder. The bird spun in the air, trying to shake me loose, but I clung tightly. When I saw my opening, I grabbed my mother's dagger and stabbed the bird in the throat.

It shrieked in pain, and I dug the potion bomb out of my sack, then shoved it into the bird's mouth until I felt it shatter. I yanked my arm free.

The bird thrashed, and I lost my grip, plummeting toward the sea. As I fell, the wind tearing at me, I felt something snap inside my chest. The darkness that filled me had broken, somehow.

It was still there, but not quite as strong. Like it had shattered and the pieces had fallen down deep inside me. Though the wind pounded me fiercely, I was at peace for the first time in days. Joy surged through me. If I was better because the potion had been deployed, that meant I hadn't caused this. The beasts had. When they fed, my dark magic exploded—not the other way around.

Oh, thank fates.

Then I crashed into the sea, the water closing around me. Bubbles flared as I kicked upward, desperate to reach the surface.

My head broke through, and I gasped, blinking water out of my eyes.

The first thing I saw was one of the giant birds. It fell into the water nearby, splashing hard.

Was it dead? Had my knife wound killed it?

The water where the bird had fallen splashed violently. Then purple light burst from the monster, and a woman appeared in its place. She rose up on a huge wave of water, standing tall and proud, the waves surging around her. Blood flowed from a cut at the side of her neck, but it wasn't a fatal wound.

A long purple dress draped her form, flowing into the waves, and her black hair floated eerily around her head. Her purple eyes glowed brightly, reminding me of Eloa.

But the similarities ended there. Pure evil radiated from the woman, and her gaze fell on me.

Terror streaked through me, and I tried to kick away. But the water made it so hard to move fast. I thrashed and struggled, but she rolled toward me on a wave. A second woman appeared at her side, identical.

The monsters were actually *women.*

And if they were able to walk on water and ride on a wave, they had powerful freaking magic.

From the sky, Ana dive-bombed them, her beak aiming straight for the women. But the witches—I was just assuming they were witches, since their eyes were purple like Eloa's—raised their hands and cast a force field that glowed white above them.

Ana slammed into it and shrieked in pain.

Holy crap.

Fear and panic surged inside me. I was far from shore. So close to them. And they were incredibly powerful.

All around me, water surged. It crashed over my head and splashed into my eyes. I coughed, choking on it.

There was so much damned water that it felt like it had become part of me. I couldn't escape it.

Do you want to?

The voice whispered inside me.

And suddenly, I realized that the water felt like part of me. New magic seemed to be welling inside me, clean magic like I hadn't felt in ages. It wasn't dark, like the magic that had poisoned me.

This was light.

This was good.

Use it.

Holy crap. That was an inner voice. Just like the one that Ana and Bree had said had appeared to them when they'd gotten their Dragon God powers.

Was I getting a new power?

As the witches rolled toward me on their waves, I tried creating one of my own. The magic was sluggish at first, slow and difficult to use. But eventually it swelled inside me.

Get me away!

The water followed my command, surging around me and dragging me away from the witches. It took me to shore, washing me up on the beach where my friends fought a bloody battle against the demons. All around, magic flew. Shouts and screams, swords and knives. But I only had eyes for the witches who were moving ever closer.

Though Bree and Ana charged them, they couldn't get past the force field.

I scrambled upright on the beach, catching sight of Caro throwing her deadly jets of water at different demons. The liquid plowed right through their bodies, coming out on the other side tinged with pink. Maximus fought behind her, tearing off heads and dodging the spray of blood. Cade fought as a giant wolf, while Lachlan rampaged in his black lion form. Ali and Haris possessed the demons, making them fight one another.

I turned back to the witches, who were nearly to me.

"Kill them!" shrieked one, directing her attention at the demons.

Holy fates. The demons weren't the bosses. The monsters were. We'd had it wrong all along.

My mind raced. How was I going to fight that force field?

The witches raised their arms in unison, and the ocean around them began to bubble. It rose up, forming a tidal wave.

An idea sparked.

Fight fire with fire. Or water, in this case.

But I wanted higher ground, away from the demons who could chop my head off while I was distracted.

Up here!

Romeo's voice dragged my attention upward. He stood on a long flight of stone stairs that led up to the steep mountainside. Poppy and Eloise stood at his side.

I sprinted up, following him, until I was out of range of the demons.

The witches' wave was huge now, aiming right for the beach and my friends. My sisters had joined the battle there.

I sucked in a breath and focused on the strange new magic inside me. It glowed brightly, feeling like a breath of fresh air compared to the darkness that had lurked there for so long. This was so much better.

The magic filled me, seeping through my veins and muscles. I could feel the ocean surging like a living thing, and I focused on it, calling it up and trying to make it mine.

At first, it resisted. The witches had too much control. I could feel their magic in the water—dark and oily, like dirty fingerprints.

I forced my magic through, imagining it as a light that spread through the water and drove out their darkness.

The witches' tidal wave began to shrink.

They shrieked, their hair floating on the air like they were electrified. In unison, they flung their arms forward.

The wave crashed onto the beach. It bowled my friends over, taking out the demons as well. They scattered on the beach, struggling to their feet. I'd mitigated the damage enough so the wave hadn't been big enough to kill, but more of those waves could do some serious damage.

Romeo patted my leg. *Beat them at their own game.*

"That's what I was thinking." I called on the magic, letting it rise inside me and fill me up.

Then I hurled it outward, forcing it into the ocean until I had control of a huge swath of it. I commanded it to rise up, and it did, a massive pillar that formed behind the witches.

It crashed down on them, driving them under the ocean's surface.

Victory surged in my chest.

I had magic!

Good magic. Pure and clean and powerful.

But the witches wouldn't be down for long. They'd rise again, as they had before. So I called on the water again. It surged tall, ready for them.

By the time the two figures rose out of the sea, there was a four-story building made of water behind them. It slammed down onto them again, driving them back under.

I tried again, calling on more water, ready to smash into the witches until they were no more. But it was harder now. I'd used so much energy already.

I didn't have enough left.

Fear made my skin chill.

When the witches rose up this time, they flew right into the sky, rising up with their toes pointed toward the ground. It was creepy as hell. They threw out their hands, and an explosion of air whooshed from them, slamming me back into the rocks.

Pain flared in my back. Through bleary eyes, I saw the witches disappear into thin air.

They were gone.

"Rowan!" Bree cried. "Are you all right?"

Aching, I scrambled upright on the stone stairs. I looked down at the beach.

The fight was over. Demons lay scattered everywhere, and a few were swimming out to sea to get away from my friends. The witches were gone.

"I'm fine!" I climbed down the stairs. The two cuts on my leg ached like hell. I'd forgotten them in the rush of battle.

I pushed through the pain, wanting to catch one of the demons to ask them about my crazy magic. There was one racing toward the water, and I picked up speed, my lungs burning as I ran to catch him.

When he was ankle deep in the surf, I leapt on him. We crashed into the water, and it splashed up around us. Desperation fueled me, and I yanked at him until he turned over to face me. I straddled him, grabbing his collar and shaking.

"Do you see the dark magic in me?" I demanded.

He coughed and sputtered, his eyes wide. "What?"

"Do you see the dark magic?" I hissed, keeping my voice low. The other demon had seen it easily.

He squinted, then his eyes widened. "Yes. But it's deep inside."

Good. That meant I was repressing it. I could physically feel the difference, but I liked confirmation. "Where is it from? Is it demon magic?"

He shook his head. "I don't know! It feels a bit old. You've had it a few years, at least. I think?"

He was confused and stressed, but the answers made sense. A few years would put it at my time with the Rebel Gods. Around the time they gave me some of their magic so I could do their evil deeds. As I'd feared, it wasn't gone. I'd suspected all of this, and now it was confirmed.

But I was controlling it. By stopping the beasts from feedings, I now had it under control.

"Can I get rid of it?"

"Maybe?" He grimaced. "That's above my paygrade, lady."

He was right. He was just a regular demon, and this was from the Rebel Gods—dark magic practitioners who were far more powerful than him.

"How am I connected to the witches?"

"I don't know!"

I believed him. He wouldn't know, but I would have to figure it out. And I could. I could do anything I had to. Surviving the Rebel Gods had taught me that. I sucked in a ragged breath, focusing on the good. Then I drew my mother's dagger and stabbed the demon in the heart, sending him back to his underworld.

Aching, I stood. The surf flowed around me as I staggered up the beach. My gaze fell on Maximus, who stood covered in blood. Apparently the battle had gotten fierce enough that he hadn't had time to dodge all of the sticky red stuff. His gaze darted to mine, concern dissipating as he saw that I was standing. Everyone else looked alive, though there were definitely some ugly wounds.

Bree and Ana landed next to me on the beach, Ana shifting back to human just as she landed.

"We did it," Ana said. "They can't feed anymore."

"Do you feel better?" Bree asked.

I nodded. "A lot better." My gaze moved toward the dark night sky. The sun had fully set and the moon had risen while we fought. "They can't feed anymore, so they won't grow stronger. But I don't think that's the last we'll see of them."

In fact, I was sure of it.

16

Two days later, I leaned on the bar at the Whisky and Warlock, our favorite pub in the Grassmarket. It was a rabbit warren of a place, full of different rooms and corridors and several bars.

The Protectorate always gathered in a little room at the front, where the beamed ceiling was low and the fireplace roaring. The gleaming wooden bar was usually manned by Sophie, and tonight was no exception.

She wore a T-shirt that said *Haggis or bust* and grinned at me as she asked, "What'll it be?"

"The usual for Ana, with a Pink Pumpkin for Bree." We came here a few nights a week usually, and she was used to our order. Ana always got pink champagne—the cheaper the better, as far as she was concerned—and Bree got whatever the cocktail of the day was. Better if it was pink with a funny name. For such badasses, my sisters sure drank girly drinks. But then, the toughest folks I knew were usually girls, so that was hardly an insult. "What's new on tap?"

Sophie leaned back and inspected the beer taps.

For myself, I was into trying different beers—the weirder the better. I'd had a Pink Peppercorn Saison once that was very good, and a banana nut stout. Maybe it was because I'd missed out on so much when I was in captivity, but it was fun.

"How about a honey Kolsch?" Her eyes met mine. "It's from Germany."

"Fantastic."

As Sophie filled our order, I leaned back on the bar and surveyed the scene. As usual, Lavender, Angus, and my other classmates were there. They made a point not to look at me. I suppressed a grin. Jealous nitwits.

We'd succeeded—mostly—with the monsters, so Jude had given me a pat on the back. More successes like that and I might actually graduate from the Academy. I couldn't believe it.

After the fight, we'd searched the old, desecrated church at the top of the mountain. There had been a nest, along with supplies for the demons and a collection of ancient golden jewelry. Greek writing decorated the walls—yet to be translated—and an unfamiliar symbol had been etched into the floor.

We were still trying to get to the bottom of it, but so far, we didn't know what exactly those witches were or what they wanted. Maybe they were gone forever, though I doubted it.

The big thing was that we'd stopped them from being able to murder, so I was counting it as a victory.

I hadn't seen Maximus since the fight, and I was itching to, but I didn't know how to seek him out. Nor did I want to make the first move, because what would I say?

"Drinks are up." Sophie's voice came from behind me.

I turned and paid. "Thanks."

She grinned and took the money. I grabbed the drinks, carefully balancing them on the way back to our little table by the fire. Ana and Bree made grabby hands at me, and I handed them their drinks.

I sat and caught Caro's eye. She was at another table with

Ali, Haris, Jude, and Hedy, and she waved. A bit of warmth spread through me. I was really starting to fit in here.

"Why are you grinning?" Bree asked.

I shrugged. "Until now, without any magic, I felt like such an outsider. Now, I feel a bit better."

Bree smiled, though she looked a bit sad, too. "I'm glad you feel better now that you're getting some of your magic, but you always fit here, Rowan. Caro and the rest aren't acting any different."

"Yeah, and Lavender's just as much of a jerk as usual, so that's the same also." Ana grinned.

I smiled at them.

"But really," Bree said. "You proved yourself with your fighting skills and your potions long ago. And you're cool. You've always fit."

"Well, I feel like I fit a bit better, now." Her words meant a lot to me, but I couldn't help it. I felt more complete.

Bree raised her gleaming pink drink. "To Rowan's Dragon God powers."

Ana raised hers. "To Rowan suppressing the dark magic."

I grinned and clinked my glass with theirs. It was still inside me—maybe it would always be—but as long as I had control of it, I would be okay.

"So you have no idea what god gave you power over water?" Ana asked.

"I don't."

"It was my first power, too," Bree said.

"There are so many gods with power over water," Ana said. "It could be anyone."

"I'll just have to hope I get more magic, and it becomes apparent which Pantheon I represent."

"It'll be a good one," Bree said. "They all are."

"Did you ever figure out who was sending you those secret letters?" Ana asked. "The ones that told you about the murders."

I nodded, remembering the moment from earlier this morning when I'd learned the secret. Jude had found me in my apartment, working on my potions. "It was Jude. Apparently, she thought I was wasting my talent and had wanted to give me something to focus on. She knew I wanted to feel useful."

"Jude does seem to know everything," Ana said.

I just nodded. Honestly, it made me feel special that she'd chosen me. That she'd noticed me.

I liked it. All in all, it'd been a very good day.

I was still thinking about Jude when my gaze was caught by a large figure standing at the door.

Maximus.

I jumped to my feet embarrassingly quickly. "Be right back."

I strode toward him, and he stepped back into an alcove in the hall. It was dark and quiet and hidden from the rest of the bar.

I followed him in. "Hey."

"Hi."

"Where have you been? After the battle, you just disappeared."

"Had to sort things out with the Order. Report on my progress and things like that."

I swallowed hard at the mention of the Order, and he seemed to notice.

His voice softened. "I didn't tell them about you."

"Good. I've got it under control, anyway."

"But it's not gone."

"No. It's not. I don't know if it will ever be. It came from my time in captivity. But it's deep inside me now, no longer causing problems. And with the witches unable to feed, I can control it."

"It's only been two days."

"I can tell. It feels different." I eyed him, feeling a mixture of attraction and mistrust. He hadn't turned me in, and I mostly thought he wouldn't. But still, it was hard not to worry. "Why have you been so nice to me?"

"I like you." He shrugged. "Pretty simple, really."

"But...why?"

"You're tough and smart and inherently good. I can see that."

"You didn't think that initially."

"At first, I didn't trust you. But then it became clear that you aren't even close to evil. Not even close. You're one of the most impressive people I've met."

I blushed, unsure of what to say. So I focused on the most important bits. He'd already said it, but I wanted extra confirmation. "So, you won't tell the Order about me?"

"I don't agree with everything they do. They're too zealous when it comes to imprisoning those who are different. So, no, I won't tell them. But you have to be careful, Rowan. No one should know what's inside of you."

"I know."

His gaze turned intense. "I mean it. They'll strike first and ask questions later. The darkness isn't you, but a lot of people won't make a distinction. I've spent enough time with the Order to realize that."

"Why do you work for them, then? You don't need the money."

"I don't. I wanted a job where I could do good for the world. And I do that when I work for the Order."

"You should work for the Protectorate." I almost slapped a hand over my mouth. Asking him to work for the Protectorate meant asking him to basically live in the same place I did, since nearly all Protectorate members lived at the castle. "I mean, they don't imprison innocent people who happen to be a little weird."

"They don't." He looked thoughtful. "But that's a consideration for another time. I agreed to do a few jobs for the Order, and I'll stick by my word on that."

I nodded, understanding. He was honorable. He wouldn't just switch it up and leave the Order hanging, even though I thought they were a bunch of bureaucratic jerks, and it wouldn't be the worst thing.

"But how are you doing?" he asked, his gaze intent on me.

"Fine. You?" It was getting a little awkward now. The attraction was there, but not acknowledged.

I felt it, at least.

Someone passed by behind me, bumping into my back. I stumbled forward, my front pressing against Maximus. He reached up to steady me, his hands gripping me around my waist.

My breath caught in my throat, and I glanced up.

Heat had drifted into his eyes, and he licked his lips.

It was as if a curtain had fallen over us. Heat fogged my mind. All I could feel was his strong hands on my waist and his chest against mine.

Unable to help myself, I leaned up on my toes. He sucked in a ragged breath, clearly debating. Then his head swooped down and his lips pressed to mine.

Desire exploded within me. I threw myself into the kiss. His lips moved skillfully on mine, and my mind buzzed. Every inch of my skin tingled.

Abruptly, he pulled back. "This isn't the place."

I blinked.

But no, he was right. My colleagues were everywhere. My sisters. Anyone could walk by.

And had I really just kissed him?

We barely knew each other. I wasn't even sure how much I liked him, or if I could trust him, no matter what he said.

I stepped away, breaking contact. I had no idea where to

look, so I glued my stare over his right shoulder. "Um, I'll see you around, okay?"

"Yeah. Sounds good."

I stepped back, and he reached for my arm, then drew his hand back before making contact. "I won't tell anyone about your dark magic. I mean that, so you don't have to worry. But you need to keep it a secret. For your own safety."

I nodded. "I will."

With that, I turned and left. I could feel his gaze on me as I walked away, and wondered why I didn't stay. It wasn't every day you felt heat like that.

Except, I didn't want to feel heat like that. Not now. Not when my life was such a mess. I needed to get my act together. And trusting... It was still hard. I liked being with him, but trusting him felt like a coat that didn't quite fit. I wasn't ready for that yet.

And he was right. I had *much* bigger things I needed to focus on. Like making sure I could really control my dark magic so that it stayed a secret. It was buried within me now, but it wasn't gone. I could let the others know about my other magic—the good stuff—but never the darkness. And my new magic needed practice. A lot of it.

It was a challenge I was up to.

I'd have to be.

THANK YOU FOR READING!

I hope you enjoyed reading this book as much as I enjoyed writing it. Reviews are *so* helpful to authors. I really appreciate all reviews, both positive and negative. If you want to leave one, you can do so on Amazon or Goodreads.

Rowan's next book will be available in two weeks. Keep an eye out. Join my mailing list at www.linseyhall.com/subscribe to stay updated and to get a free ebook copy of *Death Valley Magic,* the story of the Dragon God's early adventures. Turn the page for an excerpt.

EXCERPT OF DEATH VALLEY MAGIC

Death Valley Junction

Eight years before the events in Undercover Magic

Getting fired sucked. Especially when it was from a place as crappy as the Death's Door Saloon.

"Don't let the door hit you on the way out," my ex-boss said.

"Screw you, Don." I flipped him the bird and strode out into the sunlight that never gave Death Valley a break.

The door slammed behind me as I shoved on my sunglasses and stomped down the boardwalk with my hands stuffed in my pockets.

What was I going to tell my sisters? We *needed* this job.

There were roughly zero freaking jobs available in this postage stamp town, and I'd just given one up because I wouldn't let the old timers pinch me on the butt when I brought them their beer.

Good going, Ana.

I kicked the dust on the ground and quickened my pace toward home, wondering if Bree and Rowan had heard from Uncle Joe yet. He wasn't blood family—we had none of that left besides each other—but he was the closest thing to it and he'd been missing for three days.

Three days was a lifetime when you were crossing Death Valley. Uncle Joe made the perilous trip about once a month, delivering outlaws to Hider's Haven. It was a dangerous trip on the best of days. But he should have been back by now.

Worry tugged at me as I made the short walk home. Death Valley Junction was a nothing town in the middle of Death Valley, the only all-supernatural city for hundreds of miles. It looked like it was right out of the old west, with low-slung wooden buildings, swinging saloon doors, and boardwalks stretching along the dirt roads.

Our house was at the end of town, a ramshackle thing that had last been repaired in the 1950s. As usual, Bree and Rowan were outside, working on the buggy. The buggy was a monster truck, the type of vehicle used to cross the valley, and it was our pride and joy.

Bree's sturdy boots stuck out from underneath the front of the truck, and Rowan was at the side, painting Ravener poison onto the spikes that protruded from the doors.

"Hey, guys."

Rowan turned. Confusion flashed in her green eyes, and she shoved her black hair back from her cheek. "Oh hell. What happened?"

"Fired." I looked down. "Sorry."

Bree rolled out from under the car. Her dark hair glinted in the sun as she stood, and grease dotted her skin where it was revealed by the strappy brown leather top she wore. We all wore the same style, since it was suited to the climate.

She squinted up at me. "I told you that you should have left that job a long time ago."

"I know. But we needed the money to get the buggy up and running."

She shook her head. "Always the practical one."

"I'll take that as a compliment. Any word from Uncle Joe?"

"Nope." Bree flicked the little crystal she wore around her neck. "He still hasn't activated his panic charm, but he should have been home days ago."

Worry clutched in my stomach. "What if he's wounded and can't activate the charm?"

Months ago, we'd forced him to start wearing the charm. He'd refused initially, saying it didn't matter if we knew he was in trouble. It was too dangerous for us to cross the valley to get him.

But that meant just leaving him. And that was crap, obviously.

We might be young, but we were tough. And we had the buggy. True, we'd never made a trip across, and the truck was only now in working order. But we were gearing up for it. We wanted to join Uncle Joe in the business of transporting outlaws across the valley to Hider's Haven.

He was the only one in the whole town brave enough to make the trip, but he was getting old and we wanted to take over for him. The pay was good. Even better, I wouldn't have to let anyone pinch me on the butt.

There weren't a lot of jobs for girls on the run. We could only be paid under the table, which made it hard.

"Even if he was wounded, Uncle Joe would find a way to activate the charm," Bree said.

As if he'd heard her, the charm around Bree's neck lit up, golden and bright.

She looked down, eyes widening. "Holy fates."

Panic sliced through me. My gaze met hers, then darted to Rowan's. Worry glinted in both their eyes.

"We have to go," Rowan said.

I nodded, my mind racing. This was *real.* We'd only ever

talked about crossing the valley. Planned and planned and planned.

But this was *go time*.

"Is the buggy ready?" I asked.

"As ready as it'll ever be," Rowan said.

My gaze traced over it. The truck was a hulking beast, with huge, sturdy tires and platforms built over the front hood and the back. We'd only ever heard stories of the monsters out in Death Valley, but we needed a place from which to fight them and the platforms should do the job. The huge spikes on the sides would help, but we'd be responsible for fending off most of the monsters.

All of the cars in Death Valley Junction looked like something out of *Mad Max*, but ours was one of the few that had been built to cross the valley.

At least, we hoped it could cross.

We had some magic to help us out, at least. I could create shields, Bree could shoot sonic booms, and Rowan could move things with her mind.

Rowan's gaze drifted to the sun that was high in the sky. "Not the best time to go, but I don't see how we have a choice."

I nodded. No one wanted to cross the valley in the day. According to Uncle Joe, it was the most dangerous of all. But things must be really bad if he'd pressed the button now.

He was probably hoping we were smart enough to wait to cross.

We weren't.

"Let's get dressed and go." I hurried up the creaky front steps and into the ramshackle house.

It didn't take long to dig through my meager possessions and find the leather pants and strappy top that would be my fight wear for out in the valley. It was too hot for anything more, though night would bring the cold.

Daggers were my preferred weapon—mostly since they were cheaper than swords and I had good aim with anything small and pointy. I shoved as many as I could into the little pockets built into the outside of my boots and pants. A small duffel full of daggers completed my arsenal.

I grabbed a leather jacket and the sand goggles that I'd gotten second hand, then ran out of the room. I nearly collided with Bree, whose blue eyes were bright with worry.

"We can do this," I said.

She nodded. "You're right. It's been our plan all along."

I swallowed hard, mind racing with all the things that could go wrong. The valley was full of monsters and dangerous challenges—and according to Uncle Joe, they changed every day. We had no idea what would be coming at us, but we couldn't turn back.

Not with Uncle Joe on the other side.

We swung by the kitchen to grab jugs of water and some food, then hurried out of the house. Rowan was already in the driver's seat, ready to go. Her sand goggles were pushed up on her head, and her leather top looked like armor.

"Get a move on!" she shouted.

I raced to the truck and scrambled up onto the back platform. Though I could open the side door, I was still wary of the Ravener poison Rowan had painted onto the spikes. It would paralyze me for twenty-four hours, and that was the last thing we needed.

Bree scrambled up to join me, and we tossed the supplies onto the floorboard of the back seat, then joined Rowan in the front, sitting on the long bench.

She cranked the engine, which grumbled and roared, then pulled away from the house.

"Holy crap, it's happening." Excitement and fear shivered across my skin.

Worry was a familiar foe. I'd been worried my whole life. Worried about hiding from the unknown people who hunted us. Worried about paying the bills. Worried about my sisters. But it'd never done me any good. So I shoved aside my fear for Uncle Joe and focused on what was ahead.

The wind tore through my hair as Rowan drove away from Death Valley Junction, cutting across the desert floor as the sun blazed down. I shielded my eyes, scouting the mountains ahead. The range rose tall, cast in shadows of gray and beige.

Bree pointed to a path that had been worn through the scrubby ground. "Try here!"

Rowan turned right, and the buggy cut toward the mountains. There was a parallel valley—the *real* Death Valley— that only supernaturals could access. That was what we had to cross.

Rowan drove straight for one of the shallower inclines, slowing the buggy as it climbed up the mountain. The big tires dug into the ground, and I prayed they'd hold up. We'd built most of the buggy from secondhand stuff, and there was no telling what was going to give out first.

The three of us leaned forward as we neared the top, and I swore I could hear our heartbeats pounding in unison. When we crested the ridge and spotted the valley spread out below us, my breath caught.

It was beautiful. And terrifying. The long valley had to be at least a hundred miles long and several miles wide. Different colors swirled across the ground, looking like they simmered with heat.

Danger cloaked the place, dark magic that made my skin crawl.

"Welcome to hell," Bree muttered.

"I kinda like it," I said. "It's terrifying but..."

"Awesome," Rowan said.

"You are both nuts," Bree said. "Now drive us down there. I'm ready to fight some monsters."

Rowan saluted and pulled the buggy over the mountain ridge, then navigated her way down the mountainside.

"I wonder what will hit us first?" My heart raced at the thought.

"Could be anything," Bree said. "Bad Water has monsters, kaleidoscope dunes has all kinds of crazy shit, and the arches could be trouble."

We were at least a hundred miles from Hider's Haven, though Uncle Joe said the distances could change sometimes. Anything could come at us in that amount of time.

Rowan pulled the buggy onto the flat ground.

"I'll take the back." I undid my seatbelt and scrambled up onto the back platform.

Bree climbed onto the front platform, carrying her sword.

"Hang on tight!" Rowan cried.

I gripped the safety railing that we'd installed on the back platform and crouched to keep my balance. She hit the gas, and the buggy jumped forward.

Rowan laughed like a loon and drove us straight into hell.

Up ahead, the ground shimmered in the sun, glowing silver.

"What do you think that is?" Rowan called.

"I don't know," I shouted. "Go around!"

She turned left, trying to cut around the reflective ground, but the silver just extended into our path, growing wider and wider. Death Valley moving to accommodate us.

Moving to trap us.

Then the silver raced toward us, stretching across the ground.

There was no way around.

"You're going to have to drive over it!" I shouted.

She hit the gas harder, and the buggy sped up. The reflective surface glinted in the sun, and as the tires passed over it, water kicked up from the wheels.

"It's the Bad Water!" I cried.

The old salt lake was sometimes dried up, sometimes not. But it wasn't supposed to be deep. Six inches, max. Right?

Please be right, Uncle Joe.

Rowan sped over the water, the buggy's tires sending up silver spray that sparkled in the sunlight. It smelled like rotten eggs, and I gagged, then breathed shallowly through my mouth.

Magic always had a signature—taste, smell, sound. Something that lit up one of the five senses. Maybe more.

And a rotten egg stink was bad news. That meant dark magic.

Tension fizzed across my skin as we drove through the Bad Water. On either side of the car, water sprayed up from the wheels in a dazzling display that belied the danger of the situation. By the time the explosion came, I was strung so tight that I almost leapt off the platform.

The monster was as wide as the buggy, but so long that I couldn't see where it began or ended. It was a massive sea creature with fangs as long as my arm and brilliant blue eyes. Silver scales were the same color as the water, which was still only six inches deep, thank fates.

Magic propelled the monster, who circled our vehicle, his body glinting in the sun. He had to be a hundred feet long, with black wings and claws. He climbed on the ground and leapt into the air, slithering around as he examined us.

"It's the Unhcegila!" Bree cried from the front.

Shit.

Uncle Joe had told us about the Unhcegila—a terrifying water monster from Dakota and Lakota Sioux legends.

Except it was real, as all good legends were. And it occasionally appeared when the Bad Water wasn't dried up. It only needed a few inches to appear.

Looked like it was our lucky day.

~~~

Join my mailing list at www.linseyhall.com/subscribe to continue the adventure and get a free copy of *Death Valley Magic*. No spam and you can leave anytime!
~~~

AUTHOR'S NOTE

Thank you for reading *Gods of Magic!* If you've made it this far, you've probably read some of my previous books and know that I like to include historical places and mythological elements in my stories. Sometimes the history of these things is so interesting that I want to share more, and I like to do it in the Author's Note instead of the story itself.

First, the setting for the supernatural neighborhood in Edinburgh is a real place. The Grassmarket is a very cool part of the city located near the massive and amazing Edinburgh Castle. Edinburgh city proper contains both an Old Town and a New Town. The Grassmarket is located in Old Town, and as such, it is full of rich history and all kinds of cool places.

As you probably guessed, Old Town is the oldest part of the city and still contains much of its medieval street plan, whereas construction on New Town started in the second half of the 1700's. While New Town is a masterpiece of city planning, with broad roads and beautiful Georgian buildings, Old Town is a super cool section of the city that is ancient, twisty, and cobblestoned, with narrow alleys and underground tunnels. The perfect setting for my sort of story, frankly.

Rowan's favorite pub in Edinburgh is called the Whisky and Warlock, and it's located next to the current (and real) White Hart Inn, which is supposed to be the oldest pub in Edinburgh. It's a very cool little place with a big fire, a low ceiling, and copper mugs that dangle from the beams. I was looking for something a little bigger and more ancient, however, so the interior of the Whisky and Warlock is based on an old Devon pub called the Lydford Inn. It's bigger, with more small rooms and narrow halls. Fireplaces decorate each room, along with old wooden bars that serve all variety of Real Ale, an English staple.

One of my favorite elements of the book—The Vaults—is based on a real place. Edinburgh actually has several underground places, including the real life Vaults. They are also called the South Bridge Vaults and they are a series of chambers built in 1788 underneath the South Bridge in Edinburgh. Initially, they were used as workshops and taverns, but later they were a hotbed of criminal activity. As the vaults fell into disrepair, Edinburgh's poorest members of society moved in. By 1860, they were in such terrible shape that they were empty. Mary Kings Close is another one of Edinburgh's underground districts. It is an alley that was closed off overtime until it eventually became an underground street (buildings were built right on top, closing it in). It was occupied between the 16th and 19th centuries and in the 17th century was named for Mary King, the daughter of a wealthy advocate (something similar to a 17th century lawyer).

The Vaults as they appear in this book are a combination of these two places, set right under the castle in Edinburgh, which is located on a rock outcropping about three hundred meters high. Steep stairs from the Grassmarket lead up to the street in front of the castle.

Other history in the book can be found in the scene that was set in the Amazon jungle. Eloa's small steamship, the *Kilbourne*, is based off of a real steamboat called the *F.H. Kilbourne* that served during the Klondike Rush at the end of the 19th century. The boat was nearly identical to the *A.J. Goddard*, a boat that was mentioned in Del Bellator's series (Dragon's Gift: The Seeker, published 2016). I just love my boats, and these two in particular. The coolest part of the *A.J. Goddard* and *F.H. Kilbourne's* story is that they were carried over a snowy mountain by men, women, and mules. Albert and Clara Goddard, who built the two boats, were so determined to reach the Klondike gold fields as soon as the ice on the river melted that they broke the boats down into pieces and then took the shortcut through the mountains, hauling the pieces up and over and reassembling them on the shores of Lake Bennett, which is located at the headwaters of the Yukon River. As soon as the ice melted on the lake, they took off, shooting across the lake and down the Yukon river. Talk about determination, huh?

Other fun elements in the jungle scene come from mythology. The Caipora appeared in this book as a ghost, but depending upon where you are in Brazil, it could appear as something else all together. In most cases, however, they haunt lost travelers. The Boitatá is a mythical snake in Brazilian folklore, massive in size with eyes that could possibly blind one who looked too long. It is not always a bad creature and occasionally is viewed as a protector of the forest. In this book, however, it is definitely dangerous.

Last, while the Caipora's Den is not a historical place, the small town did play a role in one of my paranormal romances. I thought it would fun to include it in this series as well. Though the worlds of the Mythean Arcana (my romance series) and the Dragon's Gift do not formally intermingle, it's fun to revisit them occasionally. For reference, that book is called *Rogue Soul*.

I think that's it for the history and mythology in *Gods of Magic*—at least the big things. I hope you enjoyed the book and will come back for more of Rowan, Maximus, Ana and Bree!

ACKNOWLEDGMENTS

Thank you, Ben, for everything. There would be no books without you.

Thank you to Jena O'Connor and Lindsey Loucks for your excellent editing. The book is immensely better because of you! Thank you to Richard Goodrum for your keen eyes and catching errors.

Thank you to Orina Kafe for the beautiful cover art. Thank you to Collette Markwardt for allowing me to borrow the Pugs of Destruction, who are real dogs named Chaos, Havoc, and Ruckus. They were all adopted from rescue agencies.

ABOUT LINSEY

Before becoming a writer, Linsey Hall was a nautical archaeologist who studied shipwrecks from Hawaii and the Yukon to the UK and the Mediterranean. She credits fantasy and historical romances with her love of history and her career as an archaeologist. After a decade of tromping around the globe in search of old bits of stuff that people left lying about, she settled down and started penning her own romance novels. Her Dragon's Gift series draws upon her love of history and the paranormal elements that she can't help but include.

COPYRIGHT

This is a work of fiction. All reference to events, persons, and locale are used fictitiously, except where documented in historical record. Names, characters, and places are products of the author's imagination, and any resemblance to actual events, locales, or persons, living or dead, is coincidental.

Published by Bonnie Doon Press LLC

Linsey@LinseyHall.com
www.LinseyHall.com
https://www.facebook.com/LinseyHallAuthor

ISBN 978-1-942085-TB-D

18273165R00132

Made in the USA
Middletown, DE
30 November 2018